HOBOLAND

STACY NIX

STACY NIX PUBLISHING

HOBOLAND

Stacy Nix Publishing

ISBN: Print: 978-0-9989776-9-0

Ebook: 978-0-9979776-8-3

Copyright © 2018 by Stacy Nix

Cover design by Meaghan Burnett: www.MeaghanBurnett.com

Available in print from your local bookstore or online at Amazon.com.

Library of Congress Cataloging-in-Publication Data

Nix, Stacy
HoboLand / Stacy Nix 1st ed.
Printed in the United States of America

This book is dedicated to my husband John, who has encouraged me to continue on this fabulous journey of writing this book. Meaghan, who has patiently worked with me on the editing of this book. I thank all my friends and family for believing in me on this project and always being there for me. I thank my granddaughters, Madeline and Lauren, for always helping me with the marketing of my books.

PREFACE

As we watch them walk by, we try not to stare at them. We feel sorry for them, sometimes giving them money as if it makes us feel better. They are someone's child and we don't think about that at the time. Some of the homeless live their life on the streets due to situations like mental ailments, or they have hit rock bottom and can't find a way out. If you have a child, try to visualize him or her out on the streets without any food or money.

We take care of the elderly in nursing homes, unwanted babies in foster care homes, put pets in shelters, why don't we take care of the homeless?

You see them, "The Hobos" across America dressed in their finest attire. The women, in their beautiful colored blouses or sweaters, with maybe a few small holes, a few wrinkles, a little stain or oil smear, and a lovely smell of roses and sweat? Sometimes even a smear of trash. They are proud of their shoes which they find in trash cans or traded with another or even picked up at a homeless shelter. They usually have a tanned, leathery worn skin with dirt as the only makeup. The men usually have long hair sometimes tangled and dirty. Their faces come with dirt also and have unshaven faces. They have a backpack with them, and a sleeping bag, and seem to always have a blanket for night and a dog. They seem to have smiles on their faces although they are enduring a lot of hardship. The thrift stores sometimes kick them out as they don't want less desirables in their stores. They think they are too good for hobos. I know, I've worked those stores. The hobos, as I call them, with much respect, usually wear their pants two sizes too small or two sizes too large and are usually made of wool, or a fabric that would be warm for the night, as they sleep under a bridge or in a camouflage of trees. Do you ever wonder what their story is?

1

UNDER THE BRIDGE

MIKE

*I*t was a cold night and Mike was the King Hobo. It was raining hard as he was riding his bike, and he was still an hour from his home under the bridge. As he stopped at the red light he could feel the stares from the people in the cars going by. He couldn't do anything about his appearance, dirt on his face and arms. His t-shirt was dirty with many holes with a hand-written note on the back saying, "I work for Jesus." He didn't ask for money or ask for handouts. He worked hard for his money, picking up trash and cans from one end of town to the next.

He was close to a McDonalds, so he proceeded to head that way. Another red light ahead meant that there would be more people driving by in their cozy heated cars staring at him in the rain. They all had such a sad yet disgusted look on their faces. His stomach was empty, and he was feeling cold. One more block and he could get some shelter for a short time. As he approached the fast food outfit he felt a little relief. He parked his bike out front loaded with garbage bags, filled with tin cans and bottles that he could cash in for change. As he walked inside with his clothes dripping wet and dirt dripping down his arm, he felt the stares again. Shame clouded his cheeks and crept up his neck and he headed for the men's room. Alone in the men's room he grabbed a roll of paper towels, threw them in the sink to wet them and began to take a bath in the sink. The warm water felt sensational to his skin. As he couldn't do too much with his t-shirt, he took it off and rinsed it and then rang it out in the sink.

He had his bath for the day and enjoyed every minute of it. Now he hoped to get a nice, warm cup of coffee. He had a few coins and a few dollars hidden in his pocket. He had worked hard that day from sunrise to near dusk. He had to eat something soon as he felt faint. Mike ordered a meal off the dollar menu and proceeded to sit down and eat. He was getting use to the people staring at him and shaking their heads at him and looking down at him, as if he was a piece of dirt. Mike never asked for money, but he would accept it if someone offered it to him. He always said, "God Bless You," when someone handed him some coins and he meant it from the bottom of his heart. Another day, another bag of trash.

After a few hours the rain stopped, and it was time for him to head for camp. He would be late tonight and the gang might be worried about him. He hoped they might have a fire when he got to the site for some warmth. Mike headed back after a rest at the fast food restaurant. Wind pelted his face, whipping around him, making him feel like he could see shadows looming in the dark. As he arrived back at his camp under the bridge he noticed two of his camp mates, Bob and Tim, were missing. They always met together at the campsite before midnight.

Heading to the steel drum where the fire was burning beneath the bridge, he noticed his friends were gathered around to stay warm. He searched for Bob and Tim's faces. Not seeing them still, he turned to Charlotte to ask, "Have you seen Bob and Tim today?"

"No, not at all. We were going to ask you." Charlotte replied. Sitting down on the cement next to Danny. Mike hated that she looked so worn out, her dirty blond curls lackluster and her bright blue eyes dim from fatigue and stress. *Girls didn't belong living this life. Well, no one did*, thought Mike.

"I will search for them tomorrow morning. Let's say a prayer they come home tonight on their own." Settling into the conversation of the camp worry still gnawed at his belly.

When the sun came up Mike was out on his bike picking up cans and bottles from one end of town to the other. He went by the thrift store where Tim and Bob typically frequented. His search for them had yielded a camp mate who had just heard that Bob was taken to the hospital that night, and Tim went with him. Rumor was Bob had passed out. An ambulance had taken him to a local hospital, but it was a long way from camp for all of them. Mike worried more. How would they get home when they were released? Would he ever see his friends again?

TWICE A WEEK the group was invited to a large garage where a free dinner was served by a man many of the homeless called the Preacher Man. Before dinner they would listen to a man read from the Bible. Scriptures of kindness, a good life, hope, peace, and happiness. They would hear about Jesus who would forgive everyone and help the poor and teach them to be a better person. A man that loved everyone equally, no matter if you are rich or poor. As they listened to the word, they would be looking at the meal they were about to receive with a smile on their faces. If they just would listen to the man speak, and discuss what they heard, they knew that they would be fed. Often their souls would feed in the word as well. Mike loved these dinners. They were fed well, body and soul.

This evening though he arrived at his dinner with a heavy heart. The only outside person Mike knew was the preacher. He decided to ask him to check on Bob and Tim at the hospital. Approaching the preacher, he quietly asked, "Sir, I thank you for our dinner tonight and worship."

"Of course, Mike." Pausing the preacher moved directly in front of Mike, "I feel, though, like your heart isn't here tonight."

"I am afraid it is not. I need to ask you a favor, Sir."

"Sure, how can I help you?" The preacher asked.

"I have two friends in our camp. We try to keep a Godly group, and these are both good men. They disappeared the day before yesterday and rumor on the street is that they are in the community hospital. It is so far from our camp. I am hoping, maybe, just maybe, that you would be willing to go to the hospital and check on them." Before Mike had fully finished the preacher moved to the side to grab his sweater from the hook.

"Let's go, Mike. We can go check on them now."

"Now? Really? You are God's blessing, thank you!" Mikes joy infused his smile and he followed the preacher out to his car.

It had been so long since Mike had been in a car that he felt confused a slightly carsick in the preacher's little car. Thankfully, by car, the trip was short. Mike was self-conscious that his clothes had to wreak like body odor and smell of the grime of the city. If he smelled the preacher never let on. When they got near the final block to turn to the parking garage Mike spotted something that made his heart plummet. On the wall by the edge of the hospital was Tim's faded red jacket.

"Sir, please stop!" Mike said moving to open the door before the preacher fully stopped the car. Stumbling in his haste to reach Tim he stopped at the sight of his friend sobbing curled up on the wall.

"Tim, it's me." Mike said lifting his friends chin to meet his eyes. Tim was nearly unrecognizable. Covered head to toe in dirt and streaks of tears coursing down his face. Mike didn't have to ask. If Tim was out here, then it had not ended well for Bob.

"He's gone." Tim croaked his voice hoarse from his upset. "He was dead before we got here in the ambulance."

"Oh, Tim. I am so sorry." Mike said, guiding Tim up on his feet and towards the preacher's car. Mike didn't need to ask him if it was okay for Tim to ride back. He could see the worry etched on the preacher's face and the sorrow.

The ride back to the garage Tim mumbled all his last few days experiences while the preacher and Mike let silent tears fall. It was horrible. Tim spoke of the hospital's lack of empathy. That they had not done further treatments when Bob's heart had stopped as he was just a "hobo". When Tim had asked if he could bury him they responded that homeless bodies would be buried in their mass plot at the county cemetery. Tim's grief got worse at speaking of this.

"He's going to be all alone, Mike. No one who even knows his name will be there when they put him in the ground." The car fell silent as all three of the men contemplated Bob's fate.

FOLLOWING BOB'S DEATH, Mike's group decided they would try to seek an answer to their dilemma. No work, no food, no home, no real family except for themselves. They all had gone to the lowest place a person could go, and they weren't sure how to climb out. Charlotte, Danny, and he wanted more. They all did. They all deserved more than this. The next time the group went to the garage for their dinner they were surprised when the preacher pulled them aside.

"Mike, I need to speak with you. I think I may have an opportunity for you and your flock. I have seen your faithfulness to God reflected in your care of your people. That you have not once asked me for something for yourself, but you did ask me for help for another spoke volumes to your character." The preacher paused a moment before he continued. "I recently acquired some land. Ten acres not too far from here. God has granted me an idea and a means to make it happen, but I need good men of faith to lead it and guide it. I would like that to be you."

"Sir?"

"I would like to take this land and create a kingdom for the fallen. We have so many homeless in our city. I would like to make a city of homeless. But they will be homeless no more. We will make them condos, jobs, stores, food. We can help change so many lives."

Mike's shock at the proposition kept him quiet except for the occasional nod or shake of the head as the pastor laid out his idea of this utopia. An Eden for homeless to have a new start. The society would have to be rigidly moral as the property did belong to the preacher, but Mike loved that. Old time values were needed in society. He could build a Godly society that could save others like his bridge family. They could make goods and produce and sell them in the market. Before long Mike found himself agreeing to meet the preacher in the morning to look at the parcel and talk more. Excitement fused his body like a lightning bolt and he found himself unable to fall into a fitful sleep that night.

HOBOLAND

MIKE

*I*t was a beautiful day in Palm Springs, California. The desert sun was shining, and it was nearly noon by Mike's watch. Mike was blessed with a nearly perfect November day, not too hot but warm enough to keep him comfortable. Mike was peddling his bike in route to meet the preacher to see the land he had proposed for HoboLand. Mike had estimated the distance to be around ten miles and thanked the Lord that it wasn't hotter out. As Mike got close to his destination from the directions the preacher had given him he was feeling the effects of his journey in fatigue. He worried perhaps he was lost, but he decided to persevere a bit longer. The possibility of a new home and livelihood for his friends drove him on with determination. All he could see was tan sand, miles and miles of sand leading to the foothills beyond the freeway. Mike could feel the spirit of God.

Mike saw the preacher on the horizon. Slowing he hobbled from his bike to greet him.

"Hello, Mike" said the Preacher man.

"Hello, Mr. Preacher" Mike said, winded from his journey.

"Welcome Mike, please call me Pastor Luke," said the preacher. As they walked, Pastor Luke told him they would need to walk on the dirt road for about a mile to see the land, but he could see small hills ahead. Mike's heart was racing with excitement. He hadn't felt this joy for such a long time. He couldn't help but feel the spirit of God touching his journey.

Soon they arrived at their destination. The land was barren except for a well and a few camper hookup poles. There were patches of grassy weeds, proving the lands were fertile despite the sandiness of the soil. Mike felt tears threaten as he finally laid eyes on his second chance. He just knew these ten acres would be the future of his little bridge family. He couldn't explain it, it just felt blessed.

"This is my present to you and your flock. Use the land wisely and you will be rewarded. I've arranged to bring in some campers tomorrow for you and we will get started right away." Pastor Luke's grinning countenance made tears flow over in Mike's eyes.

"I'll see to it that you have water and all the facilities you need. The trailers will be temporary until we get our first building built. It would be best if you start planting food and flowers as soon as the soil is ready. Perhaps a small greenhouse to grow year-round?"

Mike nodded, still unable to voice his happiness with the changes in his life.

"Tomorrow we will meet here at first light. Please choose four men who you feel will be suitable to help you with construction. They will be fed and clothed and each given a trailer for their work."

"I think I know the perfect four, Pastor." Mike smiled thinking of his friends at camp.

"Just be warned, Mike, if they don't show up and work every day they will be let go and not allowed back. They are welcome to bring their wives and children. We will enroll the children in school and the wives will need to help us with the domestic duties here. We'll all have to help each other in the name of Jesus, we'll figure this out." Pastor Luke put a hand on Mike's shoulder to lead him back towards his car and Mike's bike.

"That will not be a problem, Pastor. I know these men will be thankful for the opportunities we are being given."

As Mike and Pastor Luke headed back, fatigue overwhelmed Mike. He didn't let Pastor Luke know that he felt weak. Thinking back Mike's last meal had been the dinner at the garage. They parted with a handshake, no papers signed or documents to settle their plan. Deciding to meet tomorrow to do the finite details.

Mike started his venture back towards the campsite. While the journey out he had been questioning and worried, now he felt the weight of the trip. The long ride back would be exhausting but his risen spirits drove him on towards the bridge.

On a regular day, he would spend trailing around picking up cans and trash and then sitting in McDonalds watching the TV while perusing a used newspaper. Today, on his way back to the site, he couldn't help himself from picking up cans along the way. He wanted to pick up enough cans for a cup of coffee and a snack from a fast food restaurant, so he could replace the money he had spent on his last meal out. His head was spinning and all he could think about was which friends from the camp he would hire. His body hummed with anticipation and feeling of belonging. Yes, yes, he was King Hobo now. Proudly, he puffed his chest to sit straighter on his bike. The good Lord was certainly answering his prayer. He called himself a construction worker, as he picked up trash, and now he was going to be a contractor again. He once had a contractor's license before. The past had not been kind to him, since he had made some poor choices during not so great times. Mike couldn't wait to be able to pen a note to his brother again. He hadn't spoken to him since Mike had ended up in the streets, and he missed him. He would be proud of Mike too.

As he neared the campsite his front bike tire suddenly whizzed air, and Mike felt himself losing control of his bike. He had been pedaling hard to make it back fast, too fast to stop easy as the tire came off the rim. Abruptly, Mike could feel himself falling free of his bike, sliding out into the road as the crunch of gravel and the squeal of brakes sounded close to his head. He slid nearly hitting the vehicle that was now nearly on top of him. Sprawled on the ground he struggled to get up.

A lady rushed from her black sports car, "Are you alright?" Worry and tears welled on her face.

Mike pulled himself up on his elbows and said, "Lady, I am blessed with God today and don't you cry for me, I'm just fine, ma'am. Dry your eyes."

Likely deducting that Mike was homeless from his unkept appearance and all his cans the lady pulled a hundred dollar bill from her purse and handed it to Mike. Mike hadn't asked her for money, but this would be just another of his blessings from God today. "Please take this. I want to pay for your bike's tire."

"God bless you," Mike replied and meant it from the bottom of his heart.

with a nod and another encouragement that he was, indeed, okay, Mike watched the women get back in her car and slowly head away. Now Mike had a flat tire, scratches up and down his arms and legs, blood coming from his knees, and he felt like he was the luckiest man on earth. He was going to take his bike back to camp and walk over to a fast food joint to get cleaned up for the day. God had blessed him with cash, so he was going to go over to the thrift store in Palm Springs to get a new outfit for tomorrow, something he could wear for the first day of his new job. Deciding he was going to pick up some shirts for himself and his crew and a few pairs of pants as well. He wanted his crew to look good for Preacher Luke tomorrow.

WHEN HE ARRIVED at the thrift shop he felt instantly welcomed. He knew the ladies that ran the shop, Malka and Stacy. When he told them about his new job they were delighted. They didn't really seem like they believed him, but when he pulled out a the bill they all looked at each other in surprise. He wanted all the shirts and pants to be in the same color. Black, if possible, if not he would go with any other dark color that they had several of. He saw an old bike tire on the wall that he grabbed with delight. Rejoicing in what a great day the Lord had made for him, he took his hoard to head back to the bridge to break the amazing news.

3

CHOOSING HIS CREW

MIKE

On the way back to the bridge Mike contemplated his decisions for crew members. Wishing he could take all of them the choices he was going to have to make would weigh on him. He knew that Danny was a good worker and young enough to work several hours a day. Danny didn't drink so he knew he could depend on him for security. Travis was a good man, he had just lost his job and his wife, so he could really use a job and some help, so mike was thinking of asking him to join them. Salvador didn't speak to much English, but he had a heart of gold. He had been working at a car wash, but it closed, and he couldn't find any other work. He had been at the camp for only a month, so Mike didn't really know him that well but the fact that he was trying so hard to get a job spoke well of him. He did come home one night with a black eye and that did concern Mike a little. Salvador said he had gotten in a fight at a gas station over money. When Mike had asked about it he said someone jumped him and asked him for his billfold and he didn't want to give it up. Mike was trusting that Salvador was telling him the truth.

One problem for him was Charlotte. She was so ashamed to be

living on the streets. She went to church to get her clothes and pretended that she lived with her sister. They all protected Charlotte, as she was a very special soul. She would cook for them and cut their hair if they needed it. They would fix the campfire, and she would cook some sort of soup, beans or whatever they had gotten from the free food bank. They all shared her meals, and sometimes that would be the only meals they would have that day.

Walking out from depositing his bounty in his cubby under the bridge, Mike surveyed the men and one woman gathered around their fire talking. With a big smile lighting up his face he approached them.

"Hi, guess what happened today?" Mike joked, knowing no one would ever guess the turn of events his day had taken.

"You got run over?" Danny ventured, taking in all Mike's scrapes and bloody spots on his jeans.

"Sort of, actually. But not before God blessed all of us." Grinning, he continued. "We have all been blessed with a second chance. A future. As King of Hobos I want to give some of you what I can, a job and a future with me"

Enthralled, Danny stepped forward, Charlotte close to his side as usual. Mike grimaced thinking of the rules of no unmarried women in camp that the Pastor had mentioned. "Well, get on with it… What are you talking about Mike?" Danny quipped.

"I have been gifted a piece of land to build HoboLand. Pastor Luke has given me and four others the opportunity to build a salvation for the homeless!" Continuing in a hurry while the others stared in disbelief, "Four of you will be welcomed in the original crew. You will need to work hard to help me build it. We will have a contractor to work under. Pastor has assured me that he is excellent and will guide us to build HoboLand well. While I was a contractor before my wife passed, he is current and up to date with the codes and such and can make this real for us!"

All Mike's friends chattered that they wanted to join Danny looked nervous though. Pulling to the side he laid a hand on Mike's arm.

"With what you said about camp, women aren't welcome if they aren't married?" Danny's gaze was on Charlotte in concern. Mike knew Danny wouldn't want to leave her. Neither did he.

"I am sorry, Danny. Pastor will not allow any women to live at the camp without being married."

Thinking for a minute Danny took off under the bridge. Mike knew Charlotte had heard their side conversation as she looked stricken. Danny didn't stay gone long. He returned looking tense.

"Charlotte, can I ask you something?" Danny's voice was tentative. Quiet and nervous.

"Yes." Charlotte whispered.

Danny sunk to one knee in front of her while Charlotte looked a bit shocked in Mike's opinion. "Charlotte, I cannot image life without you, and I don't want to. Will you marry me?"

Happiness seemed to light up Charlottes features, and she jumped up and down saying yes through her tears. Her colorful stained dress didn't detract from her beauty in her joy.

The rest of the evening was spent celebrating and planning their exciting new future. Salvador, Travis and Danny had not hesitated to say yes when he had invited them on his endeavor. Mike had been ecstatic when he had grabbed their new clothes from the bag under his bridge cubby.

The guys all tried on their new uniforms and were jumping up and down and praising the Lord. One thing about this crew was they all loved the Lord. The only problem that concerned Mike was when he had mentioned the rules stating no alcohol and no drugs Danny had made a comment, "What they don't know won't hurt them."

Upset by the idea Mike shook his head and admonished, "If you are caught one time Danny, you'll be gone and will never be able to come back." Mike hoped Danny would take heed and make sure to abide by the preacher's rules.

"Okay," Danny said, "I'm in."

Ted and Larry from camp were the unchosen ones from camp. They were trouble. Mike and Danny had asked them several times to find another camp as they weren't welcome at their camp. They were two bullies and wanted by the law. The police had chased them several times to the campsite for several different reasons. Once Ted was suspected of stealing a car, and Larry was suspected of burglary. Mike didn't want any trouble at the campsite and didn't want the police around. Although they were homeless, the good guys just wanted to be left alone and didn't want to get into any trouble.

THE NEW CREW WAS OFFICIAL, it would be Danny, Travis, Salvador and Mike. A crew of four and their dear Charlotte would even be able to join them now that she was engaged to Danny. Mike couldn't wait to get started.

4

LAST NIGHT AS HOBOS

MIKE

*T*he campfire was going out and Mike and his new crew were settling down for the night. Their backpacks were packed, and they were ready to get to the site in the morning. As Mike was the only one with transportation, Mr. Preacher Man had decided for the new crew to be picked up at the corner of Stage Coach and Highway 111 early the next morning.

It was hard to sleep that night, as the crew had doubts in Mike's plan and were nervous about the change in general. Danny had voiced another concern that he could never drink again, and Travis had worried aloud that he wasn't going to be paid for his work. Charlotte had just smiled her sweet smile and said she couldn't wait for the Lord's plan to start tomorrow. Mike knew Travis and Danny were going to need his help to succeed through their doubts. Mike was trusting in the Lord as the Lord had never let him down, even though he lived on the streets.

Glancing at his watch it was four thirty in the morning. Mike began to wake everyone. "Come on men, let's get it together. Rise and shine and let this be our new day for HoboLand."

Mike noticed Charlotte seemed scared suddenly. "What's the matter Charlotte? You were so excited last night." Mike could sense Charlotte's sadness and put his hand out to help her up.

"I am going to be the only woman." Charlotte responded.

"Don't worry, my lady, we'll take care of you," Mike said. "Dry your eyes Charlotte as this is a new day for us. We need you now. Plus, you were the only woman here with us all this time, too."

Suddenly, the crew jumped up and put their hands out to Charlotte, as if to say, we're all a family. Charlotte cried and started to shake as if she had something going on awful in her body. Danny opened a can of juice and told her to take a sip and relax. After she drank some juice, she started to relax and stop crying.

Mike said, "Charlotte, if you don't want to come we'll take you to the homeless shelter. Whatever you want, Baby." Mike put a blanket around her and told her that he had told Preacher Luke all about Charlotte, and Mr. Preacher said she would get the first trailer upon arrival today and get her choice of any location in the land. They would start their plan from her trailer. Now Charlotte was smiling and starting to get a little excited.

"Look, Charlotte" Mike said. I bought a black skirt and blouse for you yesterday, and the lady at the thrift store picked out these shoes and purse for you. I wasn't sure about a necklace for you, so she picked out this yellow scarf. Do you like them?"

Charlotte was so happy with her new clothes that she immediately started smiling and laughing.

"Come on, Charlotte," Danny said. "Hurry up and get dressed so we can get to the pickup lot."

Charlotte got dressed and looked so beautiful that all the crew whistled at her. Charlotte rewarded their enthusiasm with a little runway swirl. Proudly the crew put on their new uniforms and began to dust each other off. Charlotte had given all the men a haircut with her old, rusty scissors and the men had all shaved using an old, discarded disposable razor. They had taken turns watching out for each other as they had bathed in the public fountain in front of the local bank in the wee hours of the morning the night before using a sliver of soap Charlotte had been hoarding in her stuff. A remnant of when she wasn't homeless. It had smelled feminine and clean, but the men had been happy to be clean and ready to work. It was their last day as hobos. Tomorrow would ring in a new chapter in their lives. Mike was sure of it.

5

THE BEGINNING

MIKE

*L*eaving behind their only home for the past 3 years, the crew left to peruse HoboLand. Some of their friends had died, some had gone to other spots, and some had never been heard from again. The lucky ones had gotten ways out, like work or shelters. His crew were the very lucky ones. Thanks to Mike and Preacher Luke.

They got to the parking lot precisely on time. It was dark outside, and the air still had the cool bite of a November morning. They all stared at Mike watching the time tick on his watch.

"Don't worry," Mike said. "Someone will be here to pick us up soon."

There wasn't much traffic out, so every time a truck would approach all the crew men would look at each other with big eyes.

A big, red SUV pulled up to the curb next to where they were waiting. Mike watched as the driver got out and approached the crew with a handshake. Tall and good looking, he had on cowboy boots, jeans and a black leather jacket that seemed to emphasize his broad shoulders even more. A big smile was on his face as if he was happy to see them. Mike had half expected a dump truck and a sleazy pickup driver. He acted as if he was proud to have them in his company and treated them well, like equals. Charlotte was surprised when the stranger scooted around his truck to open the door for her. Shaking her hand and he bowed his head to her with a "Ma'am." Charlotte felt special. God was always with her and she felt his presence. They talked small talk on their way to the construction site.

The drivers name was Houston, and he was the general contractor. He explained to them had a crew, and they really needed the help of the crew to get this project off the ground. He seemed very excited to get all the trailers in and get everyone settled. He explained that there were three trailers set up now with water and all the facilities they would need to get started. The food bank would deliver meals to them until they could get their gardens and greenhouse going. Mike stated that he was in charge and he would see to it that the crew did every-thing that was needed of them. Charlotte told Houston that she was the cook and hairdresser and would keep the men fed and if his crew ever needed lunch she would be glad to fix it for them. As they approached the land Mike was surprised by the progress Houston had made the last few hours.

They decided that Charlotte would get her choice of the trailers, and the other crew members could bunk in the other one There was a brown trailer with white trim, a gray trailer with black trim, and a blue trailer with yellow trim. They didn't look too old, either. Each one was on a small lot and far enough apart for privacy despite being a camper.

6

ARRIVAL

MIKE

S tepping out of the red SUV Charlotte smiled at the trailers in the distance. They would need to ride a dune buggy to get to the trailers as they were off the main road.

There were two dune buggies parked waiting for them at the side of the road. So off they went. Houston drove one dune buggy and Mike drove the other one. It had been more than two years since Mike had driven a vehicle with an engine. He couldn't help but smile as the wind kissed their hair.

Charlotte was eyeing the blue trailer as blue was her favorite color. She was admiring that it faced east, so she could get the morning sunshine. Mike noted her dirty blond curls were mused from the ride out with Houston and Travis, but her cerulean blue eyes were sparkling with joy. She kept saying she felt like a queen.

As they approached the trailers Mike could feel his tears threatening again. He said "Thank you God, and let us give you all the thanks and praise."

Danny nodded at his side, solemn and thoughtful, "I'll never drink again Lord, and I'll never forget this gift."

Salvador chimed in his own prayer and thankfulness for God's bounty.

Mike noted something cross Charlotte's pretty tan face. Something that looked like worry.

"What's wrong Charlotte? You were so happy a moment ago."

"I have to sleep in my camper alone is all. I haven't slept inside in a confined room alone for a long time." Her face was all worry lines, "I have always had you or Danny by my side at night to keep me safe."

"Don't worry, love." Danny wrapped his arm around her side. "There is no more Howard's here... You will be safe and before long we will be married, and I will be back at your side."

When she first became homeless she slept alone behind trees and under bridges. She was approached one night by a lost cruel soul. His name was "Howard the Lion." He tried to force himself on Charlotte. She pulled out her switch blade on him and fought him off her. Then she ran down the street, clothes torn and a large cut on her eye and scratched all over her legs. Howard chased her but gave up when he saw her run into Mike's camp. And she always thanked God for Mike's camp. She hadn't been on her own long when she had run into his camp that night, but Danny and Mike had kept her safe ever since.

"I'll be brave. I am looking forward to this fresh start!" Charlotte worked hard to cheer herself back up.

Danny could still see the fear on Charlotte's face.

"Houston, do you know a preacher that could marry us?" Danny asked the man to his side.

"Well, yes, I think I could arrange that. We would love to have a wedding here for new beginnings." Smiling softly at the couple in front of him, Mike watched Houston pat Danny on the back as he turned to answer a question Salvador had asked.

Appeased, Charlotte wrapped her arms around Danny's waist. "You are a blessing Danny. I thank God for you."

"And I you." Danny smiled down into her upturned face. Mike couldn't help but feel a bit lonesome in that moment. Thinking of his own dearly departed wife and her smile, he turned to listen in to Houston.

Houston assured them that Pastor Luke would take care of this for them and get all the paper work arranged. "Okay, crew, first let's get you settled. Today will be the day for orientation and getting you all set up.

As they began to approach the first trailer, you could read the excitement on their faces.

"Lady's first," Houston said. Houston walked up to the blue trailer and opened the door for Charlotte and put his hand out to help her enter. The first words out of Charlottes mouth was, "Amen." Charlotte looked a little bit intimidated as if the trailer really wasn't hers. She a she looked into Houston's eyes with tears.

Mike and Danny and Salvatore came to her rescue. Mike put his arm on her shoulder. Danny gave her a hug, and Salvador winked at her with a smile. Mike said, "Charlotte, it's not free, you have to cook for us and still give us haircuts."

"When we get married, Charlotte, honey, I can come in and live here too." Danny's dimples flashed.

Charlotte seemed to calm down and she started looking around. There was a stove, sink, bed, breakfast table, and an indoor toilet. Pots and pans were neatly put away and towels hung on the shelf. There were beautiful colored blankets on the bed that looked so soft, and even a little radio playing the local country radio station on the kitchenette counter. Houston assured all of them that the food bank would be by at noon today, and they could fill their cabinet and shelves with food and Charlotte could plan their meals.

Next, they looked at the next trailer. This one would be for Mike and Salvatore; the third one for Danny and Travis.

Houston, ready to get this show on the road, shouted, "Okay, now crew, let's get out and see the lay of this land. Let's go over to that white trailer out in the field. That is our crew office and all of our plans are there waiting for us." They all hopped into their buggies again to go to this office and start their orientation, the driving coming easier this time to Mike. When they got to the white trailer they were surprised to see to more dune buggies parked. As they stepped into the trailer office, they were happy to see four other crew members drinking coffee and talking about plans. There were renderings on the walls, a set of plans on a desk, and a plot map on another table with plastic houses and buildings on it with a sign, Hobo- Land. To their surprise the village was gated and had street names. One was named Charlotte Lane, another was called Travis Lane, another was Salvatore Drive, and, of course, the last was Mike's Fairway. Danny was looking for his street but couldn't find it. Houston began to introduce Mike's crew to Houston's crew. To Mike's amazement, Houston's crew all had shirts on that said H.L. Construction Co. Mike didn't dare ask, but he wanted one of the shirts too. Danny asked hesitantly, "Mike? ""Are we going to get that uniform too?"

Houston heard Danny and with a smile on his face said "Come here. I have something for you."

He took them into a backroom and showed them a rack of new shirts and shorts and jeans. Each labeled H. L. Construction. Houston said, "It would give me great pleasure if each of you would take two shirts and pants home tonight, and these will be your uniforms. Let me know your shoe size and I will get you boots tomorrow. A man really needs a good set of steel-toe boots for safety on the jobsite. Work will cover it of course," with a smile he continued, "Charlotte dear, my wife will be here later to help you with your outfit. You will be special because you are they going to be our head cook and hairdresser."

Charlotte smiled timidly while she confessed, "I have my cosmetology certificate from a local college. I got it before I ended up on the streets."

"Well, now you will be able to use it!" Mike chuckled. "For more than just our old broken shears."

There was another woman working in the crew's office named Molly. She was a sweet lady that Mike hoped would be Charlotte's friend. Molly was about the same age as Charlotte, blond and sharp as a whip. They immediately seemed to like each other. Molly was married to one of Houston's crew. Charlotte was quick to point out to everyone that the Blue trailer on the plot map was hers. If anyone would ever need a haircut or a meal to just come knocking on her door and she would take care of them. Everyone giggled at her insistence to feed them already.

Mike couldn't wait to start building his kingdom.

7

BUILDING HOBOLAND

MIKE

*A*ll of them agreed to turn in for the night early, having all gotten real showers, ate full meals, and relaxed around a short fire. Clocks were set for five in the morning to get to the office by the six am start time. Mike and Salvador had played cards and Danny and Travis played their guitars next to the fire. Charlotte had mentioned that Danny's singing *Amazing Grace* had been what had finally helped her to sleep.

After a few games of cards, Mike got his yellow legal pad out and began to make notes. He was strategically planning some questions he had for the meeting the next day, such as: he wanted his men to be compensated well for their work and would they have any ownership in the property when the village was built? Did they have a corporation, and if so, who were the players? What hours would be expected of them, and how many days a week did they work? Did they have a guard at the entrance of the property to keep outsiders out?

Could he suggest some laws of this land such as no alcohol and there wasn't to be any exception to guest sleep overs? If anyone wanted to visit family they would need to do it outside until they could get a recreation room built. He always wanted them to adhere to the dress code so that if anyone from the outside such as an inspector or appraiser came in they could tell who worked for Hobo-Land. Could they put up a temporary chicken wire fence until they could put up their brick wall?

All these concerns were because Mike didn't want any of the homeless from the campsites coming in to camp in their new village quite yet until they got it set up. Once it was set up, it would be exciting to help the homeless and the street people to better their life in HoboLand. They would, one by one, take them off the streets and give them jobs in HoboLand to enrich them and change their lives. Were they going to start out with tents while building the housing or would they just start the village? What about the gardens and the fruit trees, who would co-ordinate the planting? Mike thought that he should oversee most of these things as he knew how to live off the land having grown up a farmer's son. After pages of notes Mike finally dozed off at his table, not even making it to his brand-new comfy bed.

SOONER THAN HE would have likes the alarms wailed. The food bank and another truck had delivered so much food that they had to get a separate freezer to put outside of the trailer to keep all the meat in. Mike walked over to Charlotte's camper as the smell coming from it was heavenly. Charlotte had fixed bacon and eggs, sausage and pancakes and pancakes, and biscuits and gravy for the men. Each of the men sat at

the picnic table outside her trailer with a dazed look on their face. Danny gave Charlotte a big hug and told her he loved her in front of everyone. Charlotte smiled sweetly and said, "Me too." Travis said, "Oh you two, stop it, let's get to work," as he laughed.

Mike told Charlotte to hurry up with the dishes and meet them for the first hour of the meeting. He told her that she could take the dune buggy back if she needed to go back to the trailer to fix lunch. He thought that the first day they might bring in something, as they had pizza brought in yesterday.

"Anyhow, he said let's see what the plan is, and we'll take charge of our own crew, let's call our crew the H. Land Crew?"

"Let's call our crew Mike's H. Land Crew." Travis suggested.

They all agreed unanimously and so it was, Mike's H. Land Crew. H. short for Hobo.

"Alright crew," Mike shouted, "It's five thirty. We'll meet out front at in fifteen minutes and head up to the office. Grab all of your gear and let's show them our awesome crew."

They had a meeting while eating breakfast, and Mike went over all his notes with them. He had told them that they were to follow all his instructions. He would always be open for suggestions, but he was their leader, and they had to trust in him that he would always look out for their best interest. He told them that they always had to keep an eye out for Charlotte, as this was a new venture for her, and they needed to protect her from anything that would harm her. Danny was quick to add to the conversation, that they would soon be married, and he would be living with her and so each night she would be fine. Once the fences were put up, they all would be more at ease. Charlotte was very thankful to the crew and kept saying she thought that she was the luckiest woman in the world. God was good.

As THEY PARKED, they noticed the other crew members were staggering up the stairs and into the office trailer. There were several desks set up and tables and chairs. One of the tables had a tray of doughnuts and fruit and orange juice and a large coffee pot. After Charlotte's bacon and eggs, the doughnuts that normally would have made all five of them salivate, didn't look as appealing.

"Guys, if I had known you were having breakfast here I would have made less food," she whispered to the crew.

As the room got full and everyone began to sit down, Houston stood up and smiled and said, "Good morning. Today we are going to get our supervisor, Bob, to give us a to give us an update on our plans and then we will have a question and answer period when he is through."

Bob didn't hesitate to stand up and start his orientation, "Men, and lady, we have the three acres to the right ready to go. Everything has been through planning at the city and approved. The streets have been put down by the excavating company last week, so now we are ready to get started. The first building we will build will be our one bedroom attached condos. There will be 40 to each building. Our master plan can include ten buildings that will house an estimated four hundred people. We'll have dorm style buildings for women, buildings separate for single men and another for couples with families. As it is starting out as a homeless facility, we must have separate quarters in the beginning. Everyone will be strangers. Everyone that moves in will have a job to do in this land. No one will live here without working unless, of course, they are in the elderly nursing facility." Looking over to Charlotte he continued, "Charlotte, I'd like you to work with the women in the kitchen and thrift store and flower shop that we will be setting up. And, of course, you will have your beauty shop as I have heard you have a certification in cosmetology. Mike, you'll be supervising your crew on the gardening in the beginning. Planting the trees, flowers, planting the food, and getting our money income going. The greenhouses will allow us to produce all year long to keep our community afloat. After you get some of our new hires going, you'll be supervising your crew on the gardening in the beginning. Planting the trees, flowers and planting the food and getting our money income going. The greenhouses will allow us to produce all year long to keep our community afloat. After you get some of our new hires going you'll be working with our crew and get your contractor's license again. Anyone in your crew that wants to get a license or professional certification in a trade we will help them do that. We might need to hire from the outside until we can get this facility filled, but our first hires will always be from within. We're ready to start framing today, so I'll open it up to your questions now."

Mike stood up first. "Well Bob, I appreciate this opportunity, but I was looking forward to hammering a nail or two." At that Bob and Houston couldn't keep a straight face.

Bob said, "Don't worry Mike, you are my construction crew and all your men are my top dogs for building. I am sure I can find a nail or two for you today."

"Got you," Houston said, "We have Father Donahue sending some of the farmers over to get the landscaping going. These families have lost their farms and trees due to the winter shortage of water and drought. We have been blessed to have them volunteer to help us for shelter. We will bring in more trailers for them. These men are seasoned top-notch farmers. The women are going to help in the kitchen and at the thrift stores with Charlotte. I hope I am not giving you too heavy of a load, Charlotte?"

Charlotte stood up. "I love the opportunity, but I am wondering, working for free food and board is so appreciated, but occasionally I might want to buy something personal for myself. How will I ever make a penny?"

Houston, "Oh Charlotte, don't you worry. Each of you I have brought in will have a contract today. You will have a wage for your work and a retirement plan. But if anyone breaks the rules or leaves they'll leave everything behind and can't come back again." Scanning the whole crew, Houston's gaze showed his steely resolve "You know the rules. No alcohol in HoboLand and no drugs and so forth."

"Houston, what is my title, so I will know what I am to be addressed as?" Charlotte asked.

'Okay, Charlotte," Huston said. "Head cook, thrift store manager, oh why don't we call you the Vice President of Mike's Crew? Three titles should work well for you." Charlotte laughed and smiled settling down in her seat.

Salvador stood up. "Then what is my title?"

"Your job is one of the most important jobs we have. Running the landscaping. You work with my crew and your crew and the farmers. You'll have your own office for questions, and you'll be there for them. Also, you'll order all the garden supplies and manage their payroll and write their checks for everyone in the office. We need an interpreter and since you speak Spanish, we desperately need you for that." Salvador had banking experience, so this would work for him. He dropped out of college when his parents were in a car accident and died. He seemed more than pleased.

Travis felt unappreciated and useless. He stood up and said, "What can I do?"

"Mike will need a superintendent assistant. Someone that will be a go between for our crew and your crew. Without you we will have no communication, so you must always be on your toes. You will need to be checking with everyone. Alright? Mike, Salvador, Charlotte and Danny and Travis, do you think you can do that?" They all stood up, nodding and filled with hope.

When the meeting came to an end, Houston said, "Laura has some papers for you all to sign, so we can get this going. Go get your documents signed and I'm here for you. Get to work now. Each morning we'll meet here at six for coffee and out the door by six fifteen. We'll have a meeting here each Friday at four to recap and plan. "

Danny was looking for the Preacher Man at that meeting, but he didn't come. Danny and Charlotte wanted to get married, sooner rather than later.

As Danny was leaving the room, to his surprise, the Preacher Man suddenly appeared. Danny was so excited he grabbed Charlotte by the hand and walked her over to the preacher. As they approached the preacher he held his arms out to both and gave them a hug. "I heard you two were looking for me for some reason?"

"Oh yes, Pastor, Charlotte and I are wanting to know if you would give us the honor of marrying us." Danny said.

Charlotte's face turned crimson. "Danny and Charlotte, I would be honored to unite the two of you in marriage. A man is not complete when he is alone. Charlotte you are going to be Danny's life companion. I thank the Lord for his heavenly creation of Love."

Then pastor Luke asked them both if he could pray with them and they held hands and Pastor Luke said, "Father, thank you for the love Danny and Charlotte have for each other. We thank you for your institution of marriage and the joy and sense of completion that it brings. We ask that you bless this union that will be filled for Charlotte and Danny. I know Charlotte and Danny will honor and trust in the Lord. Thank you, Lord."

Tears of happiness rolled down Charlotte clean, tan cheeks. Pastor Luke told Danny and Charlotte he would like to sit with them in a couple days to go over some pre-marital counseling, as that is required prior to the service. They happily agreed.

8

GETTING STARTED

CHARLOTTE

*T*he first few months of HoboLand flew by for its inhabitants. The first building to go up had been the thrift store. They barely had even finished hanging the doors and Father Donahue, a friend of Pastor Luke's, had brought a truck load of furniture, clothes, and sewing material, to be unloaded.

That was the day that Charlotte had found her wedding gown, it was a gorgeous gown. As she had unpacked it from her box she had wept at wanting it for herself, something she thought was slightly shameful as she knew it needed to be sold for the thrift store. She had decided to ask Houston if she could borrow it for her wedding. Houston had just smiled at her and given her a check for the cost of the dress. Telling her to put it in the cash register as her first sale at the thrift store. He had put her in charge of the merchandise and stocking her store. She thought of it as hers now. They had made sure she did.

Charlotte couldn't wait to try on the wedding dress to see if it would fit. Molly, the bookkeeper, stopped by to see how things were going. Over the past weeks their friendship had become one of Charlotte's most prized possessions.

"Oh Molly, come in and look at this wedding dress. Isn't it the most beautiful dress you have ever seen?"

Molly opened her mouth in astonishment.

"My goodness Charlotte, I never imaged the first day I met you in your street clothes the vision you would be. You look so lovely today. I am so truly happy that you are here to help us set this project. Let me see that wedding dress." Molly reached for her dress.

Charlotte didn't want to let it out of her sight. Then they both laughed like children together. Charlotte said, "Danny asked me to marry him and I want to make him so proud of me. I love him so much. He makes me feel so happy and secure, and he loves me so much. We pray together and sing together and laugh together. I believe God has given me this chance and I want to take it before it is gone."

"Oh, Charlotte," Molly said softly. "Just let me know what I can do to help you on your wedding day. I will be invited, won't I?"

"Molly, actually I have a question for you. I am wondering if you would be my maid of honor?"

"Of course! Thank you so much." The girls hugged chattering on about wedding plans and white lace.

DANNY AND CHARLOTTE ironed out the details of their upcoming nuptials. They decided on August first which would be a Saturday. Molly and Mike had agreed to be their attendants. The wedding would take place in the new garden which had come along beautifully, with roses and a waterfall. All the guests would be the new HoboLand staff, gardeners, and crew.

Their entertainment would be provided by Travis, and sometimes Danny, on their guitars. The guests from the farm could pick out any outfit from her thrift store that they wanted. Danny picked out a tuxedo that had been given to the thrift store by Father Donahue. Molly had been instrumental in helping Charlotte and Danny plan their wedding. Preacher Luke would do the ceremony, naturally. After the ceremony they would have the cake made by Vienna, one of the farmers' wives.

Charlotte had decided on a Mexican theme as she loved Mexican food and colorful art. She couldn't wait for the bright colors she felt would make her guests feel welcome and provide a great festive atmosphere. Some of the farmers were Mexican and had offered to help cater authentic Mexican cuisine. It was going to be an amazing event. She was sure of it.

9

CHARLOTTE'S WEDDING

CHARLOTTE

*I*t was a beautiful morning, and Molly was helping Charlotte with her wedding dress. They were looking for something old, something new, something borrowed, and something blue. It was an old wedding tradition that had been passed on from their mothers. Charlotte's skin felt electrified, it was such a big day in her life. She felt a bit like she wanted to run and jump for joy, but at the same time she was queasy with nerves. At the cue of the jingle of music, Molly squeezed Charlotte and with a quick, "Don't' worry Charlotte, Danny is waiting for you, honey," and left to take her seat.

As Molly walked out she winked at Mike who entered, following Molly's hug with one of his own and said softy, "Time to go kiddo! The man of your dreams is waiting. I think he is worried you will change your mind on him." Mike's chuckle warmed Charlotte's nerves a bit but not for long.

As they walked down the aisle Charlotte's whole body was trembling.

Mike felt her jitters, tightening his squeeze on her arm as he guided her up the flower strewn aisle. "Don't cry Charlotte this is a happy time."

"I know", Charlotte said, "I am just overjoyed." As Mike delivered her to the head of the aisle where Pastor Luke and Danny waited, she was in awe. Tears welled in Danny's eyes that reflected the love and vow they would share. She could see his emotions as transparently as glass, and she thanked God for the man he had brought her.

The wedding dinner was spectacular. The intricate Mexican decorations some of the wives had decorated and the festive atmosphere warmed her heart and her nerves, and she felt at peace for the first time in years. When it was time to retreat to their trailer, Charlotte was not nervous. She was excited to spend the rest of her life loving this man.

The next morning when they emerged from their trailer, late and glowing, everyone smiled silly grins at each other and started their work. Charlotte began the training of the workers for the thrift store. Charlotte busied herself after with all the displays and the window mannequins. She wanted everything perfect, like yesterday. This store would be her pride and jjoy so each of the mannequins were dressed to the nines in the windows and the displays arranged beautifully. Everything was in place and ready to open the shop. The advertising had been set. Soon she hoped people would flock to her store and make it a success.

MIKE

TIME SEEMED to fly for Mike when he was busy working with Houston. They were framing the apartments and condos now and getting the plumbing in. Both men eagerly anticipated the opening of the condos. Each evening he was studying at night to get his contractor's license back. Sometimes Mike and Houston would run into town to check their order with the lumber yard and stop at a local coffee shop for lunch. Settling into the booth Mike and Houston often talked through lunch about their plans and their ambitions.

Today, Mike was thinking more of the past than normal. He barely noticed when Houston had to reach across the table and wave his hand in front of his face.

"Mike, hey," When Mike's eyes raised back to Houston, "Man, where were you? You seemed kind of lost."

"Sorry Houston, I was thinking about the past." Mike admitted.

"I don't want to pry but—" Houston trailed off expectantly.

"Well, honestly I was thinking about everything that happened that led to me being here. Did you know I was a big-time contractor in Vegas years ago?"

"Really? Did you do any projects I know?"

"Yeah, actually. My partner, Frank and I built the Landen Casino and the nursing home on the outskirts of town."

"Wow!" Houston seemed astonished, "That build was incredible. The workmanship and design are wonderful. You should have been set for life from the proceeds. I hope you don't mind me asking, but how could you have possibly ended up on the streets?"

"Well, really it happened pretty fast. When the last check came in from the builds I was ecstatic. Living on cloud nine. I didn't realize I was being embezzled until it was too late. My partner took all the money from our accounts and disappeared, we never saw a dime of the money, or Frank, again. Of course, we had been living high and mighty. I got the worst awakening of my life when the same week I lost my house and vehicle, I lost my wife. She died." Tears welled in his eyes, threatening to spill.

"Oh, my word, Mike, I am so sorry. I can't imagine. Please forgive I asked. It is a bit ironic. I think you might have been more qualified than me for the condos." Houston and Mike chuckled at the joke and moved on to talk more about the plans.

When the men were nearly concluded, one of the most beautiful women that Houston had ever seen walked in.

"Houston!" The petite leggy redhead turned wandered towards

them. "I didn't think I would be running into you today. Aren't you going to introduce me to your friend?" Her voice was a melody that seemed to rob Mike of his power of speech, or maybe it was her brightly colored, pattered purse and the striking red lipstick? He wasn't sure. All he knew is she was stunning.

"Why of course, Marlo, this is one of our new partners, Mike," Houston nodded to Mike.

Mike stood up and shook Marlo's hand. "It is a pleasure to meet you, Miss Marlo."

Houston and Marlo cchattered on - about what - Mike didn't follow, but Marlo didn't seem to want to leave the table and sent Mike slightly flirtatious looks.

Glancing at his watch, Houston looked up to Marlo with a smile. "Well, my friend, as much as I would love to catch up more… There is work to do. We better get going. Mike—"

At Houston rising to leave Marlo rooted in her colorful purse to pull out a card.

"Mike, here's my card with my phone number if you want to get together for coffee sometime." Mike took her business card and liked what he saw. She was a real estate broker. He had worked with many realtors in Vegas, and they always seemed to negotiate a business transaction for him to make a profit in his business.

Houston was attracted to Marlo and had a lot of respect for her. She had her own real estate company. Assuring Marlo he wouldn't be a stranger they headed back to the truck to head back to HoboLand. On the way back to the job site Mike couldn't help but to question Houston about Marlo. He was fascinated by what Houston told him. She had been practicing her business for about fifteen years, and was very well respected in the industry. Mike knew better than to try to set a date with her. She likely wouldn't want to date him once Houston explained to her sometime that he had been a hobo and lost all his money.

. . .

THE NEXT TWO months saw so many changes for Mike. He felt like he belonged now. He had taken up foreman to Houston in a way, handling most of the details and keeping the work moving. He shared some of his fancier design techniques that he had learned on the casino build and the men started to respect him even more. In no time Mike Danny, Charlotte, Travis, and Salvador were running H. Land.

They no longer lived in their trailers as each moved into a private building of condos for the "managers". It was outside of the project and they had their own property close by. With their income they all got vehicles and had independence of leaving HoboLand whenever they wanted. Mike was awed by the freedom his truck gave him. They all had a choice now. They could leave and find other jobs outside of the complex if they chose to or they could stay at HoboLand and keep their jobs but live outside and train others as they came in for help.

Charlotte and Danny loved HoboLand so much that they couldn't imagine ever leaving. Danny often joked that they were "lifers". They were saving money for the future and planning on having a family. Travis said he couldn't imagine leaving either. Salvador had said he loved what he was doing and changing lives. He was happy to be the interpreter for the farmers and give back to the community that had saved his life. A few weeks back, Mike had made the journey back to Vegas for a few days. He hoped to find information on his brother's whereabouts as his letters had come back as unable to be delivered. While he was there, he had run into many of his old construction friends. Offers had seemed to pile up since then. Everyone seemed to have work for him now if he ever wanted to come back to Vegas. His family was here now though, he couldn't image leaving them while they still needed him.

MAILMAN

MIKE

*T*he rain was pouring down as Mike pulled up to grab his mail at the complex. He was still praying a private investigator he had hired in Vegas could locate his brother. So far it had been a bust. At first, he didn't register the lawyer's name marked attorney at law on the only envelope in his box. *What could this be?* Worried he opened it and sat there in shock. He was holding a check? He must have read it wrong. The six-digit sum was staggering.

Carefully unfolding the letter that had accompanied the check he read the letter. It was from his former partner's wife's attorney. She was writing to let him know that she had been searching for him for more than a year. Mike's partner had not been able to live with his deceit and his actions when he had learned it had cost Mike's wife her life and he had taken his own life. Numbness infused Mike as the words *money has been recovered* flashed in his mind. It appeared that this was the beginning of many checks to come now that Mike had left a forwarding address in Vegas. There was a phone number to call to decide for future payments. *My Lord*, he thought, *my life is so unpredictable.*

He didn't want to tell Houston or anyone about his change of fortune again fortune yet; anyone, as a matter of fact. He didn't want to lose this job that he had, and he liked his life just the way it was. He was finally at peace for the first time in so long. Now, he was thinking of calling Marlo, but something held him back. This would be his secret for now. God had blessed him with HoboLand and he would never forget that or what Pastor Luke had done for him and all the support Houston gave him when he didn't have a nickel to his name.

THE NEW CREW

MIKE

*M*ike spent one day a week with Salvador visiting the homeless. They knew where to find them under the bridges and in front of the grocery stores. Their mission was to pick five homeless people that wanted to go to work and rejoin regular society. The word had spread on the streets about HoboLand and it was getting easier to recruit. Mike had even suggested setting up an office in Palm Springs to allow the homeless to interview for positions. Houston had agreed, and they were setting it up as quickly as they could.

On this day they saw a man outside of the grocery store playing his guitar and singing for tips. Mike and Salvador stopped to listen as his song beckoned to them. This man's talent seemed to far surpass local talent. As they approached him, they gave him a brochure and asked him if he would spend a few minutes with them and get a cup of coffee at McDonald's. Maybe he could share his story with them. Their timing was perfect as the store manager had just come out and told this man there was no soliciting, and he must leave.

As the trio sat down at the restaurant for their coffee, Mike grabbed a meal for the man. He looked gaunt from being exposed from the elements and Mike couldn't help but to remember a time a few months back where he had been bathing in this exact store restroom and more of his own ribs had been showing as well.

While the man ate ravenously, Mike and Salvador told him about HoboLand and said a man with his talents could find a home there. The man was in awe. He had, at one time, been a semi-famous player in a band; however time and poor choices had landed him on the street. When he joined them on the ride back to HoboLand Mike took solace that the withered man wouldn't spend another night on the streets.

AFTER DROPPING the musician off and settling him in Salvador's old trailer, the two men headed back to the streets. They had heard a rumor of a group of homeless living under the bridge by a local Walmart and that there were women living in the camp. They decided to bring Charlotte with them on this trip so that she might help the women. After arriving at the bridge, Charlotte approached the women. She explained as carefully as she could what the opportunities were for them at HoboLand and the rules of the blessings they were being offered. The women were skeptical at first, but Charlotte showed them her HoboLand badge and the pamphlet that Mike and Pastor Luke had made for the homeless. Slowly, the three watched hope spread in the eyes of the women.

"You mean we can actually get paid? For doing real work, nothing sexual?" One of the women asked.

"No one will touch you in HoboLand," Mike stepped forward, reaching towards them to explain. Sadness crossed his face as the two women instantly stepped away from him skittishly. Something unpleasant had happened to these women as well.

"We would come, if our friend Samuel could come with us. He protects us from scary people, we can't leave him here." When Charlotte raised her eyes to meet Mike's he knew she must be thinking of Danny protecting her.

"We can bring him too. We have plenty of opportunities for you all. Where is he?" Mike questioned.

"During the day Sam works. He picks up cans to get food for us."
The younger woman responded. "But, he should be back very soon.
He never leaves us here alone after dark."

The group decided to sit down and wait for him. The two women
told them all their stories, and Mike's heart hurt for them. When an
older man hobbled into camp on a cane, Mike stood to rise. He waited
patiently while the women explained their proposition to him. Sam
seemed skeptical at first, then slightly worried. Looking to Mike, he
asked nervously, "Do you have work for a man with one working leg?"

Chuckling Mike looked him in the eye, "Not a problem sir, you
can use your hands for your work."

"We'll let you work in the laundry room." Mike continued, "You
can sit and fold the towels and help the ladies at the thrift store.
Mister, we have plenty of thing you can do for us. If you could drive a
bus you can help us a lot with the transportation."

Piling them all in the truck, he headed home. Pride infused Mike
as he showed these new arrivals their new lives. He was averaging
dozens of new members every month. His greenhouses and flowers
were flourishing. Charlotte's stores were not just breaking even, they
were prospering. The apartment condo buildings were going into
their second set now of the ten originally planned. The Lord was
providing for them all. Mike stopped at the gate and bowed his head
in thanks.

MIKE'S MONEY

MIKE

The check seemed to burn in Mike's soul. It had been weeks since its arrival and he couldn't bring himself to cash it. Somehow it still wasn't real. Having stalled so long he decided to call the attorney on the letter and enquire about it. He needed some advice on where to put his money. He wanted to keep it a secret from the crew and Houston until he had a plan. At the same time, he wanted to give back to the preacher who had saved his life and he wanted to be able to purchase part of HoboLand.

Biting the bullet, Mike called the attorney's office and set up an appointment to meet with him the next week. Sitting back, he allowed himself to reminisce of how he always wanted some land on a farm with a horse, as he grew up around horses and trained with them years ago. He thought back to Monty. He always loved that horse, he wondered where he was now. When he had lost everything, he hadn't really thought of Monty.

It was a long week while he waited for his appointment. Marlo had shown up to his office a few times. She didn't try to hide her interest, sometimes bringing him gifts of cookies or cakes. Mike was conflicted, he wanted to ask her out, but he didn't want to get involved in a dating situation yet. Marlo was lovely and smart;

someone that he would want to spend some time with. She often talked about real estate transactions she was working on and hoping that her escrows would close on time. She mentioned to Mike that she just listed some land for sale in Nevada and wasn't sure that she wanted to take that on because she didn't know anything about the lay of the land there. Her turf was here in Palm Springs. There had been some investors talking about the possibility of a casino project opportunity, but it was still just conjecture.

Mike pretended ignorance to avoid the topic but when she mentioned the name of the owner Mike almost jumped out of his chair with annoyance. Campbell always took advantage of the real estate agents. Marlo murmured aloud that she thought she would refer that listing to a Nevada agent as she was in California and thought it would work out better for her that way. Mike was relieved and hoped that name would never come up again.

Mike told Marlo he would be away for the weekend and going to L.A. for a business matter. As Marlo started out the door, Mike, in a venerable moment, asked Marlo if he could call her next week and maybe they could go for coffee.

Marlo flushed in the cheeks and her voice was quivering when she said, "Oh please let's do that."

Mike wished he wasn't worrying about what to tell her about his past.

THE WEEKEND CAME TOO QUICKLY for Mike and he was on his way to L.A. The traffic was moving well, and he decided to stop for a cup of coffee to rejuvenate him for the drive. It was nice to walk into a fast food place and pull out some money that he had worked hard for. The novelty of not being stared at anymore was nice. On his trip he was reminded often of how far the last year had brought him when he saw a homeless person on the streets.

As he approached the address on the envelope he noticed a tall sky scraper. This was it. An outsider might not have noticed the subtle shake in his hands. They would have only noted his shined shoes, well-kept attire and the smile on his face, but he was nervous. This money could change everything. What if people thought of him differently now that he might have money again? It was a miracle that he would ever be getting a penny from his old company. As he opened the door of the attorney's office, he checked in with the receptionist and waited for his name to be called. When it was he entered the office with his hand outstretched and a greeting on his lips that froze in his mouth. His Cris Flowers attorney was not a Christopher. Her subtle curves were framed perfectly in her business suit and Mike felt slightly off kilter at the shock in his hand when he shook her small but firm one. He just assumed it was a Christopher and not a Christine. When he sat up the appointment with the assistant she just said he would be seeing Attorney Flowers. Anyhow, he sat down as she started to welcome him and cut right to the chase about why he was here.

"Sir, I am glad we finally found you. I have been looking for you for a very long time. I am the attorney for Frank's wife. She was the executor of the estate when Frank committed suicide and wants to make your money yours again. She is very upset about the actions and consequences her husband's nefarious activities had on your life and we all want to put it back as best we can. Ten of the initially stolen fifteen million has been recovered in off shore accounts. Her signature in transfer back to you is all in order here. We, of course, have to pay the international taxes on the transfer unfortunately and my fees for handling, however, you will still be a millionaire when it is all said and done." Ms. Flowers voice was like balm to him. Soothing and happy. "I just will need you here a few times to do the paperwork and transfers, but it shouldn't take too long."

"I am a bit overwhelmed honestly." Mike admitted. "The hundred thousand check you sent I haven't tried to cash. Can't believe it is quite real yet."

"Oh, but it is. I tell you what. Since you have brought me nearly a year's legal fees in searching for you for Frank's wife, I would love to meet you this evening with the papers for the original beginning of the transfers. Perhaps at the grill at the Marriott?"

"That would be great." Mike said looking forward to possibly having dinner with Ms. Flowers.

"By the way, Frank left this for you. He wrote one to his wife before he killed himself as well," said Ms. Flowers handing the note to Mike.

"Mike, I hope you can forgive me for what I did to you, and your wife. I must have lost my mind to have done it. I never realized my greed could cost people their lives. I have left a note to my wife so that you are both taken care of. Please forgive me. I just couldn't go on once I heard of your fate. I know you are a believer in the Lord and you trusted him that things could work out for you, I hope this will make it so. I just wish we could have had one more cup of coffee together under better terms. Please pray for me, and I am so sorry for what I did to you. — Frank."

Mike felt his head spin. He hoped Frank would find peace and salvation with God. God could be merciful. Holding on to his own hates would eat at Mike so he decided to leave his faith with God and forgive Frank's memory. Ms. Flowers gave him space while he read but rejoined him to set a time to meet up later with the rest of the paperwork.

"Shall we meet later for the rest?" Ms. Flowers put her hand on his shoulder and waited patiently.

"Yes, let's do that. Thank you, Ms. Flowers." Mike mumbled as he headed back to his hotel in a daze.

While Mike awaited the transfer paperwork to be done he decided to open a bank account in Los Angeles to deposit all but a tiny bit of his money. He planned to take a few thousand back to HoboLand with him but the bulk of it he planned to invest with a financial planner. Mike didn't know much about investments, but he could live on the interest on an annuity at that amount for a very long time. He did know one thing for sure he would help the crew. He mapped out setting up a fund for Charlotte, Danny, Travis and Salvador so they could have a cushion for their new start in life. After all, they worked together to get HoboLand going.

He was so proud of all of them. Charlotte could have that beauty shop in the city she always wanted, and Danny could start the band he was always saying he wish he could do. Salvador could go back to school to get his degree, and Travis, well, he would need to talk to Travis for sure. He would pay the Preacher man back and see how he could help Houston. HoboLand would be his pride and joy now to share with Houston and Pastor Luke.

WHEN MIKE GOT the message to meet Christine Flowers, he headed down from his room to the restaurant. She wouldn't know it but the suit he was wearing was not originally his. He had gotten it from Charlotte at the thrift store. The irony of a millionaire wearing a thrift store suit was not lost on him as he chuckled heading down to meet her.

Mike couldn't believe how relaxed he had felt with Christine. They had fallen into conversation so easily, like old friends. He was honestly attracted to her. Not the knock him over version of attraction he had been when he had first met Marlo but the kind of enduring fascination with a person. The former wore off easy, the later not so much.

When the topic had turned from their shared passion for Hawaii to their mutual love of horses he couldn't help but feel she was a perfect match for him. She told him stories of her horse shows with her paint and quarter horses and how she co-owned a racer at Santa Anita track. He joked that he would always bet on her, and if the blush on her porcelain skin was any indication, she was attracted to him too. When the evening came to an end he couldn't help but to wish it wasn't.

AFTER MORE THAN a week back Mike still couldn't shake thinking about Christine. So many characteristics about her reminded him of his beloved wife. He tried to write his fascination with her off as residual feelings for his late wife, but he failed at that. Christine was fascinating all by herself. Mike found himself trying to think of a question he needed to ask her just, so he could call her. Finally, he decided to call her assistant and ask if she could have Christine call him at, so he could ask her a confidential question. He decided that he would give her his bank account information, so she could wire his money to him when needed.

When he had her on the phone he was thinking he would casually suggest that next time he came to town they might go to the race track as he would love to see her horse. Vaguely, he wondered if he could try to locate Monty now that he was able to care for him again. Monty had been a casualty of his situation. When he had lost everything, he had left Monty at the boarding barn. Never stopping to consider what would happen to him. He couldn't take care of himself at that point let alone save his horse.

MARLO KEPT COMING into his office and hinting that she wanted to go out. Her hints were getting less subtle, however, Mike just couldn't find the attraction he once felt. The only woman who interested him was Christine. Finally, Mike had to make it clear to Marlo that he wasn't interested in starting a relationship, not even a casual one. Marlo didn't take the news well, tossing a bit of a fit saying that she though Mike led her on to his crew.

When Mike heard this he immediately called Marlo, so he could let her know he was so wrapped up in his business that he didn't have time to enjoy life now, and while he wasn't committed he had someone else taking up room in his mind now, so it wouldn't be fair to Marlo start a relationship. After Mike's long-winded speech Marlo responded, "Mike, I appreciate your honesty. I did notice a change in you since your last trip. Let's stay friends, and if you ever need someone to talk to please call me." Assuring her he would do so if things changed at all he hung up and smiled.

13

CHARLOTTE'S SALON

MIKE

*C*harlotte was staying late working on one of her new client's hair when she saw familiar headlights in front of her shop. She smiled as Mike opened the door and she said, "Mike I have a new customer. Let me introduce you to our local newscaster."

Word had gotten out that Charlotte was the best hairdresser in town. Some of her styles had made local news and opened doors to new clients she had never dreamed of working with. She had become the new A-list hairdresser in the area. She had been puzzled when she had first started getting calls from local movie stars but weeks of them had brought her instant success. Her work spoke for itself and she was proud that her new income not only matched her husbands but sometimes surpassed it.

"I just stopped by to see if you wanted to have breakfast with me and Danny tomorrow. It has been a while since we all ate breakfast together." Mike said.

"I would love to." Charlotte replied. "I miss you when you're out of town, Mike. We need to catch up." They listened to the newscaster's stories for a while and Charlotte was so pleased at his glowing review of her haircut. Swearing she was going to have a front-page feature in the mornings newspaper tomorrow, she just laughed at his comment.

MIKE

THE NEXT MORNING Mike entered the diner and noted that the waitress that had seated them had once waited on him when he was homeless. She didn't know that Mike was once the same dingy man that she had brought in from the rain and fed him a free lunch. When Danny and Charlotte settled into the table and they began to look at the menu Mike said, "Do you remember the waitress? I bet she has no idea that we were once the homeless people on her front porch." Charlotte certainly didn't look now like she had ever been homeless dressed in a pastel pink dress with matching heels. Her long curly blond hair stood out as it was silky and shiny. Both the men had nice ironed jeans on and crisp white shirts with nice looking Ariat boots. You never would think that their past had been so desperate. Mike suggested when they finished their meal they should leave the waitress a sizable tip for her kindness in the past and Charlotte and Danny agreed.

The breakfast began with Mike asking Charlotte what was so heavy on her mind. "Charlotte, you are the best-looking former hobo I have ever met." Charlottes' face turned red and she was somewhat surprised that Mike was flirting with her with husband by her side. Mike had changed. As much as he loved his wife that died, he felt that God wanted him to move on with his life and laughing, joking and flirting, even with married friends were no longer a bad thing in his mind.

Charlotte proceeded to tell Mike that since she had hired a handful of beauticians and barbers as the shop was running at a fantastic pace and they were making a great profit each month. Charlotte had assistants that could fill in for her if needed, and Danny did most of the bookkeeping.

Mike said, "So, Charlotte, what is your dilemma?"

"Well, Mike," Charlotte said, "I have had some offers from some prominent people to do their hair and for many local celebrities in town. They would pay a large sum of money so that I could put some money aside for my future. I don't ever want to go back to that place again where we all lived on the streets and had to sleep in the dirt and pick up trash for money; no showers, no food, and freezing cold at night." Charlotte shivered at the memory. "It scares me to think of ever going back to that place. That being said, I never want to stop volunteering and working at HoboLand to help people like us to get ahead. We were homeless, but we didn't beg on the streets for money, and we picked up bottles and trash and did all we could to survive. Now, look out the window. Some of those people on the streets aren't' homeless like we were. Now, they are street people that beg for money and camp out because they don't want to work. They are different than we were. They don't want to work but love to live on the streets. They travel from town to town, beg for money, and sleep on the bus benches and in the park—" Charlotte began crying as she said, "I was saved by the grace of God when that man came to my camp and tried to rape me. When I took out my knife he still kept trying to fight me."

Danny grabbed Charlottes' hand and said, "Honey, I'll be here for you always. There is nothing to be afraid of. You are a different person now. We'll never go back to that place I promise you."

Mike started feeling his eyes mist as he told Charlotte she could do both. He told her that she had worked hard to build up her business and he was so proud of her. He told her that no one wants her to feel like she can't get ahead. "God wants you to do your best, after all he is in charge and wants only the best for you. Why don't you set up your time equally? Do your celebrities a few days and the shop a few days? Then you can see how you like that. Maybe we can take some of the profits and open another shop outside HoboLand. Then you can take a portion of the celebrity profits and give back to HoboLand."

Charlotte said, "Oh, what a wonderful idea."

"Okay, then Danny and I will start today looking for another shop." Mike thought about the fact that he would secretly help finance this endeavor, but he didn't want to say anything to give it away.

As they finished their coffee then proceeded to the cashier to pay their bill. After they paid the bill they walked over to their waitress and handed her a few large bills. She didn't know what to say but was pleasantly surprised as the tears streamed down the waitress' cheeks Charlotte knew something was terribly wrong with the woman. Charlotte put her arm around her and handed her a card. It said, "HoboLand. We are your angels in the time of need." Charlotte took her aside and told her if she ever needed anything to please call her and she would do whatever she could to help. The waitress thanked them all before they left. They told her they would have a room for her if she needed it. It turned out to be quite a heavy meeting.

14

CHARLOTTE'S NEW SHOP

CHARLOTTE

*D*anny and Mike had found the perfect little shop for Charlotte. It was in Las Palmas, Palm Springs. On opening day her clients were lined up in no time and again she had a flourishing business. She needed someone to answer the phones and to set up appointments, so she immediately thought of the waitress at the diner. Not sure what she would find, she decided to drive over to the diner to see if she would be interested in the job. The waitress name was Betty and she was so thankful that Charlotte had remembered her. She was now starting to show she was pregnant. She knew she couldn't keep up the waitress job as it was hard to be on her feet all day.

"Hallelujah," she said, "I can quit this job right now. No more people yelling at me for bringing the wrong dinner or not liking the cook's meal. No more carrying those heavy trays and no more working unit midnight. No more mopping the floor and wiping the tables." Little did she know that her act of kindness to Mike and Danny had been returned to her. Someday they would share that story with her. Now Charlotte had two shops. Danny worked the crews and did Charlottes' bookkeeping. Danny still didn't have a street named after him and wondered at that some evenings with Charlotte.

ONE DAY while they were all eating together Danny asked Mike "How come everyone has a street in HoboLand named after them but me?"

Mike laughed so hard tears were coming down his cheeks. "Danny let's go for a ride I want to show you something."

They drove back into HoboLand and Mike drove out past the business building and out by a dirt road. There was a new development going up with 40 condos, and the streets were just being finished. There was a grocery store being built, but not quite finished. Mike took Danny into the storage room of the new grocery store and asked him if he could give him a hand with something that he needed to hang out front. They go into the storage room. There was a large sign covered with paper and tape. Mike asked Danny if he could help him carry it out front and hang it. They proceeded to uncover the sign. To Danny and Charlotte's surprise the sign said, "Danny's Grocery Store."

Mike said, "We thought you would never ask. If you would have asked in the beginning, we would have told you." They had a good laugh at this.

Danny was joking but he put his fist to Mike's face. As he pretended to swing Mike turned the wrong way and Danny's fist went into Mike's face. In shock, Mike stepped back feeling the sting of Danny's fist a little to late to save him from what would surely become a shiner. Mike began to laugh and said, "I guess I deserved that for not telling you sooner." Charlotte giggled as they went back to the shop and Mike put some ice on his eye.

AFTER A WEEK the black eye disappeared. Everyone that knew Mike and Danny knew that it was an accident, but it was hard for Mike to explain to strangers that it was a friend that put his fist in his face but the three of them all got a good laugh from trying to explain.

IT HAD BEEN a few months since Mike had seen Ms. Flowers. She still hadn't left his mind though. He had no desire to seek out Marlo or any other women, so Mike decided to tell the crew that he would need to take a few days off to get some personal business done. He wanted to see if he could spend some time with Ms. Flowers, if she would still be interested in that. Mike called Ms. Flowers and asked her if she would want to go to the race track to watch the horses run. Ms. Flowers seemed surprised by his call but eagerly agreed to meet him at the track that weekend. Ms. Flowers belonged to the Jockey Club as an owner, so she had a reserved box for all the races and always went to the owner's lounge restaurant to celebrate the day.

WHEN MIKE LEFT Palm Springs he planned on spending a few hours in Los Angeles, so he packed his clothes for this adventure accordingly. Christine called Mike to ask if he would be interested in riding some horses the day after they went to the race track. Mike knew what he would need and what to buy. He had left all his jeans at home, so he would need to buy some...

Friday Mike was off to LA and then on to a hotel near the track. Ms. Flowers also had a condo near the rack track. Mike stopped in LA at a country shop he had heard about to see if he could find some riding gear. Mike was excited to have the opportunity to spend some time with the second love of his life, horses. Mike didn't want to go overboard with his tack, but he wanted to be prepared to ride whatever Christine had available. Mike and his old partner Frank typically had ridden four days a week in Vegas. His mind wandered again to Monty and wondered what had become of him.

Mike met Christine at the entrance to the restaurant. He had cleaned up and dressed to shine in his new favorite boots, jeans, and his new dress shirt. He had found an amazing fun silver buckle for his belt. Charlotte had styled his hair for him before he left, and the shorter cut accented his tan masculine features. Christine took his breath away. Not only did she have a brilliant red hat she had a shimmering tight long dress that looked like it was painted on her. Dresses like that should be illegal for what they did to a man's blood pressure. Her long red gloves and matching red clutch kept him from touching her skin as he offered her his arm. She looked almost shy for a moment. Her silver heels lifting her diminutive height to nearly his nose.

"Ms. Flowers, you are breathtaking. Literally." Mike said as he guided her to their table. They had barely ordered their drinks when Mike's phone sounded off in his pocket and noting the caller ID was Charlotte he quickly said to Christine, "I am afraid I must check this. It is my best friend's wife. She never calls me, so it must be urgent.". Charlotte usually didn't call Mike unless it was an emergency, so he didn't hesitate to slip from the booth to the side of the room and click the answer button.

"Hello?" Mike couldn't quite make out the sound, but it sounded strangely like a sob on the other end of the line. "Charlotte?"

"Mike… Thank God. You must come back. Right now, please. It's Danny." Charlotte's borderline hysteria cut him to the quick as he tried to process what she was saying through her sobs. Catching little pieces that Danny had been in an accident he told her he was on his way and to call if she had any news at all.

Rushing back to the table Ms. Flowers looked up from her menu with a creased brow.

"I am so sorry, Ms. Flowers. Danny had been in an accident. I have to go back."

"Here, let me drive you down. I can come right back. You are too distraught to drive all that way alone." Agreeing as Mike felt like a shell of the man he had been before the call from Charlotte he agreed to it and they got in her car to head back to Palm Springs.

15

DANNY

CHARLOTTE

*C*harlotte couldn't imagine a deeper fear. She pleaded with God, with the doctors, with Danny's prone body itself to please pull through. They had told her that Danny had been in a car accident. He had been on his way home from HoboLand when a drunk driver had crossed the double lines and hit him head on. Charlotte could see all the markups on his medical chart at her side and the nurse's murmurs told her it was bad. Worse than bad. Nausea swamped her. She had only shared the news with Danny yesterday. News that they were going to be parents. He was going to be a father! He couldn't lay there with broken ribs, broken legs, and internal hemorrhaging so badly they used words like "poor prognosis" and "less than good outcome". He was unresponsive. Charlotte pinched his arm hoping he would open his eyes and tell her to quit. Danny was the strongest man she knew. He *had* to make it. She had calmed some from when she had frantically called Mike and the others. Now only the sound of the life support could be heard at her side. They told her it would be touch and go. The night would tell them if he would pull through. He had to pull through. It was Danny. *Her Danny*. There wasn't any other option. Smoothing his hair next to the bandage covering his head wound she bowed her head and pleaded with God.

All that was left to do was wait. Wait and pray and hope. So, she would stay by her husband's side she vowed, they would have to make her leave.

MIKE

THE RIDE back was long and agonizing for Mike. To pass the time he decided to share his story with Ms. Flowers. He wasn't sure she would see him in the same light once she had heard about his time on the streets, but he prayed she would. He told her of all of it. From Frank and his business to all the funny antidotes he could think of that told her about Danny. Danny's kindness, his compassion, his protective side. Ms. Flowers had more compassion than anyone he had ever met. When Mike bowed his head in prayer she had pulled over for a moment to join him in it.

They had found a common ground, "God." It seemed that they had never discussed before their belief in the Lord and now it was the most important subject they had ever talked about. You see Ms. Flowers loved the Lord with all her heart and Mike did also. Mike told Christine about his t-shirt he had written on to keep up his morale on the streets, it had said "I work for Jesus" on the back. The ride back to Palm Springs changed something in them both.

Mike couldn't say what, but he knew it was changing and she seemed to feel it too. They weren't far from Palm Springs when Mike jumped from the ringer on his phone. It was Charlotte. Mike knew. Just as he had when he had seen Tim broken on the side of the road. Danny was gone. Mike answered the phone nearly on auto-pilot. He listened, barely hearing the words. His best friend was gone. He cried, huge sobbing tears, even as they pulled into the hospital and Christine shut off the engine wrapping her warm clean scent around him.

She held him as he wept for his friend and his family. Once the worst of the sobs passed Mike was slightly embarrassed and slightly uneasy. She had seen him at his worst. Heard the worst about him. Quickly he hurried from the car as she mentioned something about having a friend help her bring his truck back later. He wasn't truly listening as he felt nothing but pain and worry. When they parted he knew without a doubt he had left part of his heart with her.

WHEN HE FINALLY GOT CHARLOTTE HOME THAT night he opted to sleep on her couch in the condo. She hadn't been alone since she had married Danny. He wished more than anything he could take her pain away. Salvador and Travis had been by her side every moment. It was even harder than being on the streets again. He knew he would have traded everything to get Danny back, but God doesn't work that way. Mike struggled over the following months to get Charlotte to work, eat or sleep. She seemed to be wasting away in front of their eyes. Her bright blue eyes had lost their sparkle.

Finally, one day Travis and Mike had found Charlotte laying in the grass outside her apartment sobbing. Mike watched Travis kneel and tell Charlotte that if she was scared to sleep alone he would sit on her porch all night if she wanted, but she had to do something for the baby. Her swollen belly was growing, and she wasn't taking care of herself.

The course of the following month brought about significant changes. Wherever Charlotte was as was Travis. He forced her to eat, to come to the office or salon each day, and he had even taken up residence on her couch. They were all sitting around the lounge one night when Charlotte gasped, her hands flying to her belly in wonder.

"Mike, Travis, I just felt the baby move!" Suddenly it was like she was seeing her belly for the first time. She caressed the mound that was the child she and Danny had created with wonder.

"If it is a boy it is going to be a Danny, like his father." Charlotte smiled, and Mike's heart healed just the tiniest bit.

16

ROUND TWO

MIKE

*I*t had been nearly a year since that fateful night they had lost Danny. Mike had stayed in contact with Christine but the baby coming had kept him from leaving Charlotte for too long. Soon after baby Danny was born, he had gone on a few day lunch trips with Christine, but he had been nervous to make any big moves. One day, Christine must have decided to move their relationship along as she called him to request a redo on their ill-fated race track date. Mike agreed, while that day had started with so much promise, he couldn't help but to look forward to more promise for the future.

The day of his date Mike felt the nerves eating up at him as he pulled out his jeans and called to book a hotel next to the track. Deciding he might need more help with the success of this date, he bowed his head in prayer that nothing horrible would thwart their budding relationship again. The trip down went blissfully fast as he was lost in his thoughts. As he pulled his pickup into a spot near the front he looked over to see Christine gracefully unfolding herself from her car parked close by. He stopped to appreciate the long line of her shimmering silver dress.

She had again paired it with some beautiful silver kid gloves that she was slowly pulling off to put in her clutch as she noticed him her smile warmed his heart. He felt a little weak with the vision she presented in her gown and prayed he would still be able to carry on a coherent conversation. As they settled into dinner, he was wondering at her being the most beautiful woman he had ever met. Maybe not Marlo's stunning red-haired looks, but Christine's classic beauty was the kind poets wrote about.

Unlike their other lunches something was different about this one. She seemed almost shy to him. When Mike brought up that he didn't know much about her personal life. She told him that, like him, she had once been struggling through a tough past. She told him of her struggling years when she had divorced her abusive husband and moved into the dorms at her law school. More days than not she would only have cereal or ramen noodles for food, but she had persevered to get her degree. While her practice had only recently started paying larger dividends, she had striven through a great deal getting it up and running. When she asked if he would like to see her racer run today, he grinned and said, "Of course!"

Holding out his arm for her to taking him to see her mare in the claiming race coming up he felt a spark of electricity run up his arm at her touch. She was electrifying, mesmerizing. He froze in place as their eyes caught, he knew she had felt the same chemistry from the quizzical look on her face.

"I am so glad you agreed to come today, Mike." She added softly.

"Me too, I wouldn't want to be anywhere else." Mike squeezed her hand and chuckled softly, "So show me your mare. I can't wait to see her run."

The race was about to start, and all the horses were in the holding paddock that staged the racers before they ran. Christine pointed out a gorgeous large dapple-gray mare sporting bright purple and a white number two on her side. She was magnificent, and he felt the tug of longing for Monty more keenly at watching these beauties get ready to run. Mike watched as they loaded her mare into the gates and found himself holding his breath, waiting for the bell to sound. At the buzzer his heart was in his throat as he watched Christine jumping up and down beside him cheering on her mare and yelling at her jockey. He couldn't help but to love watching her. As they turned the final stretch her pretty mare was in a nose in nose battle with an odds favorite racer. Mike sent up his own cheer as her mare pulled ahead to take the race by a whole length.

"Oh, my goodness!" Christine grabbed Mike in a huge hug. "That was her first race! Her first win! I have to run down for the winner's circle shots, come with me?" Christine's excitement was infectious.

"Naturally, let's go down." Mike watched in amazement as she was swarmed by a herd of people, her mare received her winnings. As the trainer came up to introduce himself to Mike and congratulate Christine Mike felt a sliver of recognition. He knew him. His name was Charles Sebastian and he was a well-known trainer, often working with horses in Vegas as well. Mike had met him years before when Charles had still been working with reiners in Vegas during the off season from the track.

"Mike?" Charles held out his hand to enthusiastically shake it.

"Charles, wow it has been years! How are you?" Charles told him of his recent successes from Vegas to Santa Anita.

"It's been so long. Did you ever get Monty back from Frank?"

"Monty from Frank?" Mike asked confused.

"Yeah, when you disappeared Frank heard you hadn't paid board on Monty. He bought him from the sale that the barn owner sent him to." Pausing Charles realized this was new news to Mike. "You didn't know?"

"No, I had no idea what happened to Monty. Thank you, Charles. Do you happen to know what happened to him when Frank died?"

"Well, yes, he is at Frank's brother's ranch last I heard. He's not a spring chicken anymore but he can still do a sliding stop like no other. You should call Frank's brother and see him." Mike agreed. He couldn't wait to try to see if he could get Monty back. Even while Mike still had Monty on his mind, Christine invited him to go riding with her in the morning. He readily agreed, enthusiastic to spend more time with her and couldn't wait to be in the saddle again.

THE NEXT MORNING Mike tossed his saddle and cinch in the truck pushing his Stetson further on his head. He was ready for a long ride with Christine. He picked her up at six thirty and they headed to the ranch. They were like two eager children off on an adventure. When they arrived at her barn, she asked her assistant to get the horses tacked up and ready and bring them around to the front arena, so they could ride a bit before going out on the trail. Mike laughed at her obvious deduction that he hadn't ridden much and said, "Come on you don't need a groom, you have me. I can saddle up any horse and prefer to ride in my own saddle if it fits your horses. What rides do you have available here?"

"I have a few pleasure western mounts. One old naughty reiner that can be a handful." Christine replied.

"I'd prefer the reiner if you don't mind."

"Are you sure? He's a bit, well, sensitive. He also doesn't get out as much as we would like, so he can be a bit forward as well." Christine still looked concerned.

"I have been riding reiners since I was six. Pretty sure I can still handle one naughty old gelding, even if it's been a while." Mike's wink and bright smiled proved his confidence.

Looking happy but slightly nervous Christine muttered, "You're a Godsend. I thought this might be a walk only trail ride." Giggling she tossed the geldings bridle to him and they both settled into tacking their mounts.

Mike was a bit in love with his mount. The older gelding was still very zippy for a reiner pushing twenty, but his sliding stop left nothing to be desired. He was responsive and moved off his leg at the slightest hint of a cue. Mike lost himself in his ride and conversation with Christine. She was so witty, fun, and generally amazing. She had made him laugh so hard that he was often near to tears of joy. When the evening was ending Mike couldn't help but consider the idea of possibly buying a ranch of his own. It had always been something he had wanted to do. At first his wife hadn't wanted one, but she was not around anymore and somehow, he thought Christine would love it. When had his life plans started to always include Christine?

He didn't know. But he didn't mind either.

When Christine had offered him to bring a horse to her barn in LA he decided he might want to think more on this. Perhaps, she and the horses were his future?

17

BACK TO HOBO LAND

MIKE

*M*ike's condo in Palm Springs sometimes felt a bit small to him now. He would still go to HoboLand each day to supervise all the contractors and work with Houston. He loved that Charlotte was still running her shop at HoboLand and at her select boutique salon and slowly but surely getting over Danny. None of them would ever forget Danny, but time seemed to be healing her wounded heart. Mike couldn't help but notice that Travis and Charlotte seemed to get along very well and were spending more and more time with each other. He always seemed to be by Charlotte's side and helping with her son, Danny. Sometimes, Charlotte would take Danny to work with her and all the hairdressers would help her take care of him during the day, Charlotte could afford daycare now but preferred to keep Danny close by as he was growing way too fast. There was a girl that worked at the thrift shop that moved in with Charlotte and she loved to take care of Danny. They sometimes jokingly called her "the nanny". Mike noticed Travis was over nearly every day without fail and would help do anything Charlotte needed. He had built Danny a crib and dresser and seemed to love him like his own son.

Charlotte and Travis would take Danny to the park and play and play and laugh so much together, it healed Mike's heart to watch her happy again.

Danny Jr. looked just like his dad and sometimes that was hard for them all. One day over coffee Travis had confessed that he wanted to marry her. He was worried how the others would take it, but Mike assured him that it would be amazing, for all of them. Charlotte was becoming fond of Travis and tried to stay away sometimes because she thought people would think it was too soon after Danny's death too. Mike had to tell Travis, while it wasn't the same as her and Danny, that no one would begrudge them both happiness.

18

DOUBLE WEDDING

MIKE

*E*ach date Mike and Christine went on Mike felt his love for her grow. He found himself checking his phone nearly constantly, and Christine never being far from his mind. He had broached the subject with her a few times about buying a ranch in Vegas and she was all for it. He told her he couldn't ever fully leave HoboLand as it was his passion as well, but he needed more of his own. He saw Christine much more regularly now as she helped pro bono for HoboLand's legal department. He couldn't image his life without her in it anymore, and he didn't want to. One night they all decided to go out to dinner together at one of Palm Springs best new restaurants. Pastor Luke and his wife, Houston and his wife, Salvador, Charlotte and Travis joined Christine and him at dinner. The view from the restaurant was breathtaking.

While they were all together, Travis stood up to move to Charlotte's side.

Quickly glancing at everyone's quizzical glaze he looked deep into Charlotte's beautiful blue eyes and knelt to one knee. Christine covered her mouth in awe as the pastor's wife's eyes teared. "Charlotte, I love you, will you take me as your husband? I know it is not just a decision for you, but I want you to know I want to be part of Danny Jr.'s life and bring him up just like Danny would have. I want to teach him to play the guitar with me, show him his dad's favorite songs, play football and basketball, and anything else he ever wants. I want to be there for you both, forever. Please say you will be my wife?"

Without any hesitation Charlotte said, "Yes, yes yes—" as she launched herself from her chair into Travis' outstretched arms.

Congratulations abounded as the men clapped Travis on the back and the women oggled the beautiful diamond solitaire that Travis had slid on her ring finger.

Settling back in the table Mike leaned over to Christine to joke, "If I hadn't been a hobo at one time I would be asking you the same question, Christine."

"What does that have to do with anything?" Christine asked with an odd look on her face.

Feeling kind of sheepish Mike said, "Well, I am not good enough for you."

"Mike, you are more than good enough for me. Your past doesn't make you less of a man. It makes you more. Look at what you guys have built in HoboLand? The lives you save daily, thinking so little of what you have to offer is sad." Christine's tone made Mike believe in her sincerity. She really thought he was her equal in every way?

"So, if I had asked you to marry me tonight?" Mike asked, he was worried about what her answer would be as if he was asking her for real.

Her face lit up, making her eyes even more alluring, "Mike, my answer is yes. It has been yes for a long time. If you're ready to ask I am ready to tell you yes."

Travis having caught the last of this leaned over and laughing in mirth, "Well cowboy, you had better ask your woman today as well then, before she smartens up and they change their mind on us!"

Laughing, Mike dropped to one knee to follow Travis' example and proposed simply to his love. With tears in her eyes she smiled her consent and suddenly conversations about weddings to come with the talk of the rest of dinner. Somehow, their conversation had circled them around to a Vegas double wedding and both couples had agreed it was an excellent idea. Now all they had to do was iron out the details.

19

WEDDING PLANS

CHARLOTTE

I *can't believe I am having a double wedding in Vegas.* Charlotte thought about her upcoming nuptials with worry. Ms. Flowers was a gorgeous, professional woman, did she really want a simple Vegas wedding? Charlotte worried perhaps she had gone along with the plan at dinner simply because Travis and she had suggested it.

On the other hand, Ms. Flowers clearly wanted all her friends at her wedding and Charlotte, Travis and the rest of their HoboLand family were her friends. During planning the wedding, Ms. Flowers and Mike had suggested so many items since they both had lived there before, knew the area and the vendors. There was a small chapel that both Mike and Ms. Flowers had both said they loved and when she showed Charlotte the pictures online she had to agree as well. It was lovely, smaller and perfect. They all decided to go up a few days early to make sure everything was set and to enjoy the city. Charlotte couldn't wait. It would be her first time in Vegas.

. . .

CHARLOTTE STARTED SETTING up plans for her help to take over while she was gone. She would close the out of town shop for a week and have her friends from HoboLand run her thrift shop. She had ladies that could take over her shop while she was gone, and everything seemed to fall into place. Mike was getting his crew ready to take over for him while he was gone, and everything seemed to be running very smooth. Ms. Flowers said she didn't have any appointments for the next two weeks as she was volunteering at HoboLand to help with any legal papers that needed attention, so she was ready to start packing. Travis had helpers working under him, so he had no problem in getting away. It wasn't long before they headed to Vegas, Charlotte's nerves were high, but she was so excited about her future.

They had decided to stay at the MGM Hotel as Mike had stayed there many times before and liked that location on the strip. Ms. Flowers and Mike took the route through Amboy. It was once a major stop alone the famous Route 66 according to Mike. From Palm Springs you can save about 45 minutes in travel time to Vegas using this route, but you don't ever want to do it at night as if you take a wrong turn you would be lost for sure. What was once a boom town in 1926, today is much of a ghost town. In 1973, HWY 40 opened which bypassed Amboy. There isn't much there now besides a closed school and a closed gas station and Roy's motel and Café. It has been said that Movie companies use the area for photo shots for movie. Mike had been telling Charlotte all about how he was looking forward to showing it to Ms. Flowers thanks to their shared love of history. Charlotte couldn't help but to think of how romantic that would be.

Charlotte and Travis loaded up Travis's truck and headed out via the more direct route, the freeway. Charlotte had one of her friends taking care of little Danny while they were gone.

When the met up at the chapel they could hear *The Hawaiian Wedding Song* by Elvis Presley. The inside they noticed it was so decorated with flowers and bouquets and stargazers all around. It was so enchanting they all just looked at each other and knew this was the perfect chapel for their weddings. It held about fifty people in the event any of their HoboLand friends like, Houston his wife, and any of the crew that would want to come.

Soon another Elvis song came on. *Love Me Tender, Love Me True.* Charlotte's eyes welled with tears of joy. Travis grabbed her hand and said "Charlotte, I promise I'll never forget Danny. He will always be with us. You know, Charlotte, he would want the best for Danny Jr. and I promise to be the best father to him and I would love to adopt him, if you want to, so he can have our same last name. We'll never let him forget Danny." All of them agreed and Mike decided to lead a prayer for Danny's memory to be close to them in this time of joy.

MONTY

MIKE

*T*he following morning, they got up early, having decided the night before they would stay an extra day to try to locate Monty. It was a long ride outside of Vegas to Frank's brother's farm, but Mike was anxious to see Monty. Frank had sometimes talked of his brother's place being huge, but it was the biggest Ranch they had seen in a long time. Mike was hoping to come to an arrangement to bring Monty back home. As they walked into the barn they didn't see many people in the aisle. There were several horses in the barn, and in the arena to the right trainers were working cutting and reining horses. Mike didn't see Monty anywhere. Mike heard someone approaching and turned to see an older version of Frank in a way. Erik stopped at his side to ask, "Are you Mike?"

"Yes, you must be Erik? You look so much like him." Mike tentatively shook the older man's hand.

"Yeah my little brother and I were pretty close in the looks department. I am so sorry for what Frank did to you. If it helps, when you disappeared, Mike, he sent Monty to me. He bought him from the slaughter auction the boarding barn sent him to because of the back owed board and told me to keep him here safe for the day you came back."

As much damage as Frank had done to his life, at least his old friend has stuck true to one thing. He had protected his horse. Erik told Mike they rode Monty once or twice a week to keep him in shape, but generally he was just loved on by the barn crew. Leading Mike back to the separate "retiree barn" that was lovely; huge stalls with private fans and private chain link paddocks behind each individual run in barn. Monty had been kept in one of the stalls reserved for Erik's national level retired horses.

Tears spilled over as he walked to the fence and Monty tossed his black mane at the sound of Mike's voice, "Monty". He must have remembered Mike as he took off at a dead gallop to the fence line to meet Mike. Mike opened the gate and hugged his gelding with tears streaming down as he ran his hands over his horse. Monty looked great. Older, his coat had some streaking of gray in the face and was no longer the pristine black of his three-year-old self that Mike had originally trained, but his friend was still his friend.

Turning to Erik he asked, "How do we do this? I know you have had him for years, but I would like him to come home for good."

"Well, with everything Frank took from you I want this to be the one good thing he gave back to you. I can haul him for you to wherever you would like. This is my number—" handing Mike his card with his cell number on it, "Just call me when and where you want him, and we will get him to you. I am so sorry for my brother. I miss him every day. I just wish there was a reason he had done what he did." He had to agree. As horrible as his life had been for a while, some of the best blessings he had ever received had come from his days on the streets. God wanted him to forgive this man and Frank's memory, he could feel it. Hate would just cause his internal wounds to fester so he chose to forgive. It was for the best.

They planned to bring Monty back to Christine's ranch, and Mike wasn't sure it was real until Erik and him pulled into the ranch with him a few hours later. Charlotte and Travis had driven out to meet them, so they could meet the famous Monty. When they pulled in and settled Monty into his freshly bedded stall, Mike turned to Charlotte to say, "Charlotte, Danny had promised me that he would get Monty back for me. I feel like Danny would be happy for me. I once told Danny that I would teach him how to ride Monty, so now I'll teach little Danny someday." Mike hugged Charlotte and Travis before they headed back to HoboLand for the night.

21

HOBOLAND'S PROGRESS

MIKE

*A*s the crew always had, they still visited the homeless in Palm Springs picking up those they could. They took in as many as they were able, as HoboLand was thriving and so far, they had been able to save hundreds from life on the streets. It had become a whole new little city with its shops, greenhouses, and products being produced. Mike had rarely had to enforce their rules as most had been happy for the opportunity and had adhered to their ordinances. Occasionally someone would be caught trying to bring drugs or alcohol back to the site, and it was dealt with quickly and efficiently.

IT WAS a circle of beautiful harmony. Everything was coming full circle. Recruiting homeless and adding onto their growing HoboLand had become routine. They had developed an orientation program and job matching system so that the new recruits would feel more comfortable and better suited to their new jobs. All the new recruits started out with shared trailers and after they were there for a few months, they would get moved into the condo development.

Of course, some of the recruits didn't make it as they wanted to go back to the streets and not work or couldn't overcome certain obstacles. There was a mental help facility along with a small medical clinic onsite to help those with physical and mental disabilities that would normally limit their ability to assimilate to the new society of Hobo-Land. They had opted to make a wing next to their senior living facility which now only housed people who were mentally or physically disabled and kept them safe. Mike's crew had made sure they were treated with the utmost dignity and very well cared for.

22

MARRIED IN VEGAS

*F*inally, the day arrived for the double wedding. They had settled on twenty-five guests from HoboLand and their closest families outside of HoboLand. The wedding was soft, breezy and perfect. There wasn't a dry eye by the end of the ceremony. After the ceremony they had a great reception in the MGM ballroom. A former friend of Ike and Tina Turner's, named James, came came as their entertainment and brought down the house with an outstanding performance.

Houston's speech had put them all in a whimsical mood when he told the story about the first time he had picked up Charlotte and Mike. To look at the difference today in tuxedos and the ladies in beautiful gowns. He couldn't hold back his tears of joy when thinking about the changes changes had brought for them.

MIKE MOVED into Ms. Flowers ranch, but they had decided to look for another place closer to Palm Springs. Palm Springs was too hot for horses and there wasn't proper land there except for an area called Clancy Lane in Rancho Mirage or a ranch subdivision in South Palm Springs. They were going to look out in Corona and some other areas where they could get a lot of acreage and access to good trails for riding. They wanted to get a house with a guest house and some casitas for the Ranch Hands and some casitas for their HoboLand crew to come out and visit. Mike could now provide very well for himself and Ms. Flowers, and he wanted to pay back Pastor Luke and Houston and invest in HoboLand. Mike's investments over the last two years had yielded very impressive results since he hadn't handled the money at all. Honor, dignity, a good future, and most important values in life. He wanted to teach people to help others in need and work hard. He was so proud of Travis, Salvador, Charlotte, and little Danny. He had the best family anyone could ask for. And a wife that loved him even though he was once a poor hobo.

Mike would never forget where he came from and couldn't believe how blessed he was to have gotten his money back. It took a lot of hard work. He had to humble himself and had a lot of prayers. Yes, his prayers were answered in huge ways, but he was humble and thankful for the blessings. Mike would do many orientation speeches, and he would tell them how he, too, was once homeless, himself and how he would ride from one end of town to the next all day long picking up cans on his bike to get cash for money for food. How he would take a shower at McDonalds or anywhere he could find water. He stressed if you want to get ahead keep your nose clean at HoboLand, follow the rules, work hard and God would provide their future here.

23

CHANGES TO COME

MIKE

$\mathcal{I}$t didn't take long for Mike and Christine to decide to sell her ranch. They just needed to find something suitable for their forever home. Mike told her about his friend Marlo and suggested that Christine call her to set up an appointment at some possible places. When Christine had called, he had heard Marlo's excitement all the way through the phone. They set up a time to look at all the possible options close enough to HoboLand.

A few days later Mike opened the door to Marlo, stunning in her black leather skirt, leather boots, and beige tight fitting silk blouse, covered up with a very tasteful neck warmer. Her jewelry was tame, and she looked very professional. Although, her red ruby lipstick was questionable. Her smile was warm and genuine as she put her hand out for a gentle handshake. Mike invited her in and introduced her to his wife. Christine smiled at her and eyeing her small framed body slightly uneasily. Once they shook hands and talked a few minutes about Christine's ranch the tone changed significantly as both women were all business and the underlying current seemed to melt away.

For the ride around Christine's ranch, they piled into Marlo's SUV.

She had started talking all about the comparable properties to Ms. Flower's ranch and what could be expected at sale. Soon however she turned to Mike, "How have you been? I still think of you occasionally, you know." Her tone left no doubt she was subtly flirting.

"Marlo, I didn't realize you and my husband used to date." Christine put in, her tone cooling a bit as though staking her claim.

Mike thought it wise to defuse the situation a bit, "We didn't exactly date, Christine. We had mutual friends in Houston and went out for a cup of coffee a time or two."

Thankfully Marlo pulled up to the stables and that point ended the conversation before Marlo could say more. Houston had told Mike that Marlo was with someone now, which had been part of the reason that Mike had been okay with using her as his realtor. Surely, she wasn't still attached to him?

MIKE AND CHRISTINE discussed her property sale that evening. She had inherited the land from her dear late father that had died in an airplane accident when his plane had disappeared in the Bermuda Triangle. Mike didn't like the idea of her using her proceeds from the farm to purchase what would be their house, so they agreed to split the down payment of the new farm evenly but the net proceeds from the sale of her ranch would stay Christine's. During their discussions that night about property, Mike could tell something was bothering Christine. "Hun, what is the matter? You have been kind of sullen all day."

Christine looked up from her spot next to the window to murmur, "That Marlo is very pretty."

Mike glanced up from what he was doing, knowing something wasn't right here. "Yes, she is. But, love, you know you're the most beautiful woman I know, right?"

Then she asked him, "Did you ever kiss her on your dates?"

Mike smiled, wrapping his arms around his wife and placing a reassuring kiss on her lips, "No, love, when I first saw you I knew she wasn't the one for me. I didn't lead her on. I told her I only had eyes for someone else. Then I fell head over heels for you." Then he said, "Honey, if you are not comfortable with Marlo we will get another real estate agent"

Sighing and snuggling closer in the haven of Mike's arms Christine just smiled and said, "Never mind. For a moment I was a little self-conscious. I love you."

"I love you too, more than anything. You are my whole world. Please don't forget it."

IT DIDN'T TAKE Marlo long to find extraordinary equestrian property. It was lovely and in an irreplaceable location. One of the parcels available was set for up to a twenty-stall horse barn with pastures, storage barns, a manager's home, and professional massive, indoor arena facility which had been used to train top Grand Prix show jumpers. You could ride off the property on the 30-mile trail system. There was so much to this property that Mike couldn't believe it was available. Marlo had told him the owner recently had a heart attack, and his wife passed away last year and he just wanted to move on with his life.

Mike decided to take a ride up to look at the property in person. He was pretty sure this was the perfect home for him and Christine, but Marlo had also told him about a few others. He called Marlo to set up a day of looking at them all.

THAT EVENING CHRISTINE had told him she had an idea of what they wanted to do with the profits from her land. She wanted to use most of the money to purchase the parcel adjacent to HoboLand to start a HoboLand Ranch. She wanted to hire all homeless people for the crew to build and expand it with Mike guiding them and open the facility to train and resell show horses. If they taught their crew of former homeless people to train horses, she could pick horses up that were homeless themselves like Monty had been at that meat auction and they could give both the horses and the homeless people a second chance at once. The sales of the trained horses could support and expand their program, and she could help to make the same kind of difference Mike had. Mike loved the idea. It was perfect! They spent half the night planning their next steps and laughing together when Christine stopped and put a hand on Mike's arm.

"My dear, don't you think you should tell your friends about your past before you were homeless? Salvador mentioned to me today that none of the guys knew much at all about your previous life other than you occasionally telling them about Monty?"

"I didn't tell them before I learned about my money because I was ashamed to have fallen so far. Then I met you and I didn't want to tell them I had it again."

"Mike, I don't understand why you won't let your friends know all of you. Your money before hadn't kept you from becoming a great man. Your money now doesn't stop you from doing great things. I think you need to trust your friends and tell them the whole truth about your past and your present." Mike knew she was right. Keeping these secrets and his money from his friends had been something he had been so worried about for so long. If he wanted grace in his soul, he needed to lessen the burden and trust his friends not to think less of the man he is or the man he was.

"We will have a meeting and tell them together." Mike agreed. "Tomorrow we will look at ranches first, though, and find the perfect ranch for us."

Wrapping her arms around his waist Christine leaned in to hug him close.

MARLO HAD PICKED out four ranches that she thought might impress them. The trip was uneventful with a truce of sorts with Marlo on her best behavior which relieved Mike. She even mentioned something about her new fiancé. Surprised Mike asked who she was engaged to and Marlo gave him a saucy little smile when she said that it was the same Campbell fellow that Mike had been worried about possibly taking advantage of Marlo. After his shock wore off he wished her the best and meant it.

Mike and Christine were so impressed with what they saw they were speechless after their showings. Christine had loved seeing all the horses, meeting all the ranch hands and musing aloud of the opportunities if each place was theirs.

Mike and Ms. Flowers found two ranches that they were visualizing Monty and Christine's racers in the barn. He couldn't believe it. The first ranch was the one that the man had a heart attack and his wife died and just wanted to get out of the property. That was still their favorite. Marlo told them that if that was the one it probably would be sold very fast as the sales price was well below market value. They knew it was a marvelous buy and a gorgeous property and the price was astonishing for what they would be getting. The land was set up so that some of the property could be subdivided sometime if the wanted to sell off some parcels later and make a profit from their investment. It didn't have a pond, but it had a swimming pool and a hot tub and tennis courts. Mike joked that his cowboy inner self needed to learn tennis. Mike called Houston to ask about the cost of building some casitas and they were very pleased with his initial numbers. Returning home, Mike decided to talk it over with Christine but he was sure he knew the course God was guiding them to.

Now they could also sell their condo' and keep working to build HoboLand. "My Lord, Mike, we can start HoboLand Two like we dreamed about. Think of all the people we can help if we do this." The more money we have, the more we can spend on the homeless and HoboLand. We can build that HoboLand Church we have always talked about."

"Our future looks so blessed, my love. I can't wait for the new place. Maybe we should buy a pony for Danny Jr.?

"Yes! Yes! I will ask my groom to start looking for one. That would be perfect!" Christine agreed.

24

FOUNDER FRANK

MIKE

*T*he next day Mike decided it was time to fully share himself with his family and friends. He called everyone together for a meeting in his office at HoboLand. Everyone was chattering together animatedly. Charlotte looked festive in one of her sundresses while Danny played contentedly on her lap. Pastor Luke, his wife, Houston, Salvador, and Travis were all gathered around talking amongst each other.

"I called you guys here as you are the closest people to me, and we have talked about so much. I have kept things from you all." Mike told them about what his life had been like before the streets. His money, Franks betrayal, and his wife's death. Christine was at his side holding his hand even when he wept at parts of his story. He continued to tell them about how he met Christine and the staggering amount of money he had now, again. He told them of his plans for wanting to buy the lots adjacent to HoboLand to build more and the new riding and training barns." When Pastor Luke looked at him with an odd look in his eye, Mike started to worry.

"Mike, there is something you should know. While the church

bought the land, the money that paid for all of it, including the land was from a single organization. It is owned by one Frank Mills. That isn't possibly the same Frank Mills you were talking about was it?"

Mike couldn't catch his breath. It didn't take a rocket scientist to figure out that most of the money Frank had stolen was sitting laid out at his feet. His partner had taken his whole world from him, but Frank had also given him back more than he could have ever dreamed of.

"Are you sure?" Mike asked the preacher.

"I am positive. His wife herself is the one that endowed the church with this projects financing, she said it was something he asked of her in his final letter to her."

Mike fell back into his chair and let the years of resentment wash away. *Look where I am now.* If Frank hadn't gotten greedy and then repented would he have met these amazing people? Would he have his wife and the wonderful work he had now? The Lord had surely blessed his way and helped to guide him to this place and these people.

The first few days Mike worried if his relationships may have changed from the news, but life at HoboLand went on as normal. His friends loved him just the same and he was the happiest he had ever been. Plans for the new HoboLand additions were laid out with Houston and his crews and everyone was jolly and lifted. There was even talk of Charlotte setting Salvador up with her sister since they had reconnected after the passing of her mother a few months back.

EPILOGUE

YEARS LATER

$\mathcal{H}$oboLand was now operating in full force. They had a fully functioning small village of their own complete with a beauty shop, flower shop, grocery, post office, church and the new facility across the road was where he could be found most often. There each day, Mike found his purpose in helping to train horses with his crews. There was a satisfaction to training the horses and finding them the perfect home. Each sale's income went further to support the formerly homeless trainers and gave them something to connect with and love. While he had lost Monty a few years after the facility opened, Mike had found a daughter of Monty's from his younger stallion days and now a line of Monty's graced their paddocks. Each with the same wonderful brain and brilliant ability.

Everything in the store was produced at HoboLand except for household supplies. The fruit trees were flourishing, and all the crops were abundant, their greenhouses allowing production in all seasons. There were over fifty apartments hundreds of condos built and there was still room for expansion since they had bought the adjoining lots. It was amazing what their shared vision had yielded. Homelessness in the local area was at an all-time low and people came to HoboLand to buy their products to support their cause. Christine and Charlotte had arranged a marketing campaign with the local medias and it had been picked up nationally and Mike's crew had gotten offers of investors for new HoboLands in other cities. God had delivered hope for so many.

MIKE AND CHRISTINE WANTED CHARLOTTE, Travis, and Salvador to be a part of HoboLand Two also, so Christine drew up a document assigning them a part ownership of HoboLand Two and created a trust for Danny Jr. for when he became of age. At twelve, he was he was currently a handful, running his family ragged but they loved him with no end. He was by far the best rider at the ranch. Travis had adopted him and there was often talk of Charlotte and Travis expanding their family. Mike and Christine hadn't ruled that out either.

Next to the gate to HoboLand there was a sign. The sign Mike and Pastor Luke had posted for Frank's wife in memory of Frank. It read, "Blessed be our founder, Frank Mills".

AUTHOR'S NOTE

My husband and I spent time, through a church group, feeding the homeless and the less fortunate. We would meet at a large rented garage in an industrial area and serve them dinner. There were about five homeless people in our group. Sometimes only three would show up for dinner. Our routine was to meet and greet them, sit down and read a scripture from the Bible, and have a small group discussion. Then we would lay out a wonderful dinner, furnished by ourselves and loving members of the church. They would show up at five, one by one.

Sometimes a woman would come. I loved it when she would come. I could go through the sweaters with her and pray with her. I prayed I could help her get through her time of need. My husband would read the Bible to them with all the patience in the world. One night we had a mentally ill homeless man that couldn't concentrate on the reading of the word and he just wanted to stand up and shout, rant and rave. My husband proceeded to read from the Bible until he just couldn't get the attention of this poor lost soul. Finally, John my husband, smiled and closed the Bible and prayed for this man and then we proceeded to lay out the dinner. We were pleased to fill the room with scripture, hope, laughter and fellowship.

One special homeless man, I'll call Mike, was a delight. He said he worked in the construction business. He would ride his bike around town each day to pick up bottles and cans for money. He was a pleasure to be around and had a great vocabulary. He liked his life and had adjusted quite well to sleeping under the bridge, he called camp. He had a very serious schedule every day for his work. He would come to our dinners and seemed to enjoy the fellowship. He would participate in all the discussions and he wouldn't be in a hurry to eat or a hurry to leave.

It would be heart wrenching each night to leave the garage, knowing we were going home to our warm cozy bed, while our new homeless friends were going to the bridge. It was certainly hard to see a woman leave with the men to sleep under a bridge.

We would give them literature and phone numbers for assistance. We did what we could to help them. I would be lying if I didn't tell you that I often thought of bringing them home with us. At night I would find myself at bed time thinking of them and wondering if they were okay.

_____ Stacy

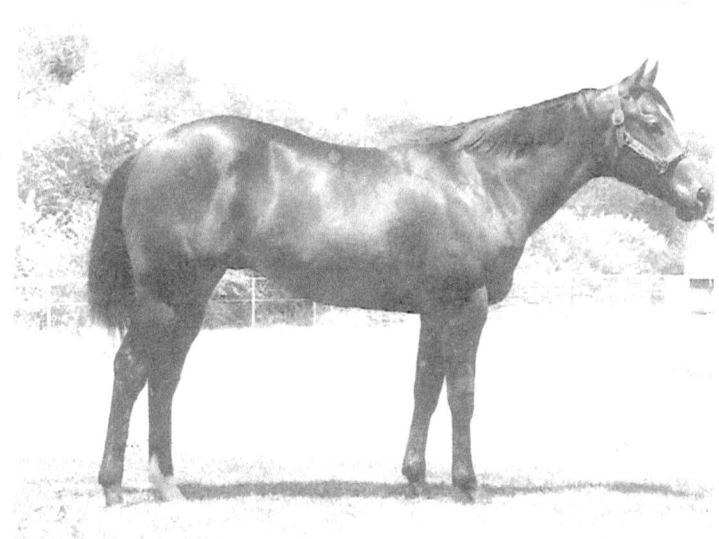

ACKNOWLEDGMENTS

I want to thank the Church in Palm Desert that asked John, my husband, and myself to feed the homeless in a garage. I thank the thrift store in Palm Springs that I volunteered at to raise money for the homeless by working in the shop and modeling for them in fashion shows with my dear friends, Malka and Elaine. I thank the wonderful characters in the book, some were completely fictional and some were based on real people and modified. I thank them for bringing homelessness to the reader's eyes in hopes that this book may someday be a blue print to help the unfortunate. I thank my friends, Donna P. and Patti S. for being my cheerleaders and sharing my books to the world. Terri G. for always wanting to help with editing and Lori J. for sharing my book with her mother Pat, and Christopher, my son, for giving me encouragement on this project, and Mike G for suggesting an audio of the book. The Nix family for all their support. Also a special thank you to Austin, Lauren and Maddie for your support.

I want to thank John, my dear husband, for his support, guidance, encouragement and love on this journey.

ABOUT THE AUTHOR

Stacy Nix was born in Long Beach, California. She has been a freelance writer for years and writes from the heart. When she isn't writing she is raising money for the homeless with, "People Helping People". Stacy and her husband and two dogs reside in Palm Springs, California.

f

www.ingramcontent.com/pod-product-compliance
Lightning Source LLC
Chambersburg PA
CBHW022040170626
46808CB00003B/1299